Men of Tortuga

by Jason Wells

A SAMUEL FRENCH ACTING EDITION

SAMUEL FRENCH
FOUNDED 1830

NEW YORK HOLLYWOOD LONDON TORONTO

SAMUELFRENCH.COM

ISBN 978-0-573-69648-0   Printed in U.S.A.   #29062

IMPORTANT BILLING AND CREDIT REQUIREMENTS

All producers of *MEN OF TORTUGA* *must* give credit to the Author of the Play in all programs distributed in connection with performances of the Play, and in all instances in which the title of the Play appears for the purposes of advertising, publicizing or otherwise exploiting the Play and/or a production. The name of the Author *must* appear on a separate line on which no other name appears, immediately following the title and *must* appear in size of type not less than fifty percent of the size of the title type.

In addition the following credit *must* be given in all programs and publicity information distributed in association with this piece:

Developed through the New Plays Initiative
by Steppenwolf Theatre Company, Chicago, IL,
Martha Lavey, Artistic Director, David Hawkanson, Executive Director

World Premiere by Asolo Repertory Theatre, Sarasota, FL
Michael Edwards, Producing Director, Linda DiGabriele, Managing Director

MEN OF TORTUGA was presented August 6, 2005, at Steppenwolf Theatre, Chicago, Illinois, as part of the First Look Repertory of New Work. The Project Director was Edward Sobel. The cast and crew was as follows:

AVERY . . . . Thomas Edson McElroy
TAGGART . . . . Darrell W. Cox
KLING . . . . Keith Kupferer
MAXWELL . . . . Matt DeCaro
FLETCHER . . . . Ben Viccellio

Director: Amy Morton
Set Designer: Keith Pitts
Lighting Designer: JR Lederle
Costume Designer: Ana Kuzmanic
Sound Designer: Martha Wegener
Dramaturg: Sarah Gubbins
Stage Manager: Deb Styer

MEN OF TORTUGA opened November 17, 2006, at Asolo Repertory Theatre, Sarasota, Florida. The cast and crew was as follows:

AVERY . . . . Douglas Jones
TAGGART . . . . James Clarke
KLING . . . . David Breitbarth
MAXWELL . . . . Eb Thomas
FLETCHER . . . . Paul Molnar

Director: Greg Leaming
Set Designer: Marjorie Bradley Kellogg
Costume Designer: Michele Macadaeg
Lighting Designer: William Peeler
Sound Designer: Matthew Parker
Stage Manager: Juanita Munford

CHARACTERS

TOM AVERY - 50s or 60s. Subscribes to a benign, somewhat detached managerial style; but may have hidden reserves of ferocity.

TAGGART - 40s. Self-taught military scholar. His self-confidence and sense of authority are convincing for a while, but may not withstand scrutiny.

JEFF KLING - 45-55. Aggressive and excitable, sure, but it's worked for him so far.

KIT MAXWELL - 70s. A stern, old-fashioned aristocrat. A long, cynical life has made him sullen and insular.

ALLAN FLETCHER - 25-35. Smart, dedicated, and very polite. But then, he's selling something.

NOTES ON PUNCTUATION

The slash (/) indicates the point at which an overlap begins. That is, the actor with the next line will begin speaking at this point.

Ellipses (...) never indicate overlapping lines. In every case, the speaker has, for whatever reason, left his own speech unfinished.

To Karen

Scene One

(**AVERY**, **TAGGART**, **KLING**, *and* **MAXWELL**)

AVERY. We have a man in a room…

TAGGART. Yes.

AVERY. A high office. In a tall building…We have one spot from which…

KLING. A nest.

AVERY. *From* which…a person could shoot. We measured the distance: One hundred…seven…?

KLING. …Fifty-seven / yards…

AVERY. …Yards, and some – …?

KLING. Something…

AVERY. We have it exactly, but – it's written elsewhere, as / you…

TAGGART. Sure.

AVERY. For obvious reasons, / I think.

TAGGART. Sure. This is through *glass*, this shot.

AVERY. Yes. Not *bulletproof*…

TAGGART. No. But thick glass. It's an office building. A skyscraper…

AVERY. Yes.

TAGGART. Hm.

AVERY. Hm.

TAGGART. Okay. The distance is difficult. Very difficult. But I'm assuming we're talking about the very best equipment…

AVERY. Oh, yes. / Anything.

KLING. Equipment is not a / problem.

TAGGART. Right. But at that distance, a pane of glass, even a *regular* pane of glass, will affect the trajectory of the bullet. This is going to be a skyscraper window, which is, like, a half-inch *minimum* thickness of reinforced glass. With a Light-Fifty and a tungsten-core round, you might punch through, but you can't keep the trajectory.

AVERY. A Light-Fifty.

TAGGART. Yeah, and a tun– That's a rifle.

AVERY. Sure.

KLING. *(to AVERY)* It's a rifle.

AVERY. Sure. But it's, but it's just *glass*, right?

TAGGART. Mmmmm…

AVERY. Could it affect the…trajectory – Could it affect it that much, really?

TAGGART. At *that* distance? I don't know how much you know about this…?

AVERY. Well, *nothing*. You / should assume…

KLING. I've done some / reading…

TAGGART. Okay. Well, it's not like you see in the movies. You can't just put your man in the crosshairs and let fly. Not at *that* distance, certainly. You have to calibrate your scope to the *arc* of the bullet. You have to know the *weight* of the bullet. You have to calculate wind direction and wind speed.

AVERY. I see.

TAGGART. You have to calculate…

AVERY. Uh huh…

TAGGART. You have to calculate *humidity*…

AVERY. Yes.

TAGGART. All of these things affect trajectory. But a pane of *glass*…

AVERY. I see.

TAGGART. It's *possible*, of course. Don't get me wrong. But you would have to decide if the risk is worth such a wild shot. Is the glass *tinted*, even? What if they pull the blinds? Is it day / or night?

AVERY. *(to KLING)* Is it tinted?

KLING. It's *slightly* tinted, but I looked right in. You can see half the room. It's / daytime.

AVERY. I didn't think about the blinds, either.

KLING. I don't even know if they *have* blinds. I think it's one of those – Oh, what would you call it? I think it's like tinted on the *inside?* And it reacts automatically to the light? But they're gonna want the *view.* I'm sure. I mean…Yeah. They're gonna want a nice view.

TAGGART. Anyway. In answer to your question, given the restrictions you've offered, I would have to say that you have a low chance of success.

AVERY. Would you be uncomfortable if we broadened the parameters of your…*purpose* here…a bit?

TAGGART. I don't think so.

AVERY. You…?

TAGGART. I mean I wouldn't be uncomfortable with that.

AVERY. Okay. Thank you. So…in that case…What could you see us doing to improve this scenario?

TAGGART. I won't ask who the target is…

AVERY. You shouldn't assume it's *anyone.*

TAGGART. Of course. We're developing an abstract.

AVERY. Of course.

TAGGART. But I would have to have a sense of the level of security.

AVERY. Let's say "top." *Top* level.

KLING. I think that's safe to say.

TAGGART. I assume the hide can't be closer.

AVERY. The hide?

TAGGART. The *hide,* the…sniper… / hide.

KLING. Snipe…sniper…*nest.*

TAGGART. Hide.

AVERY. Oh. Closer? I just don't see / how.

KLING. This is really the only practical / position.

TAGGART. And your target is absolutely limited to just this one individual?

No one else in the room should be…uh…harmed.

AVERY. Well. We, uh…we, uh…

KLING. Hm.

AVERY. We…?

MAXWELL. Of course not. Absolutely not.

AVERY. Yes.

TAGGART. Then you have to find another place. You have to get him in the open.

AVERY. That isn't going to be possible. Believe me. This one opportunity has presented itself, and hoping for another, well…Without going into details, I can tell you that this just has to be the time and it just has to be the place.

TAGGART. Okay. In that case, you would have to be willing to accept failure.

KLING. What if we got rid of the window?

TAGGART. Okay…

KLING. I mean, hear me out on this: What if we placed explosives on the *outside* of the window, where they wouldn't be discovered, around the edges of the window, and we blew up the window right before the bullet came in? Do you see?

TAGGART. Your guy would duck. He would be under the table as soon as he heard the / explosion.

KLING. No, but you could *time* it. Electronically. So that the explosion was at the exact same time as the bullet. You could determine the travel-time of the bullet and create some sort of *switch*…that would start a, a *timer*, that would set off the explosion so that he didn't even have time to *flinch* before…you know, he's *hit*.

TAGGART. The shock wave from the explosion would alter the trajectory of the bullet.

KLING. It's a big window. If the explosions were small, relatively small, up in / the corners…

TAGGART. The window wouldn't just *evaporate*. It would just be *starting* to shatter when the bullet came through. The bullet would still have to pass through shattered glass, or flying glass…I don't think so.

(pause)

AVERY. Then a rifle is not the answer.

TAGGART. I think that's true. If this has to be the time and this has to be the place, then I think it's your *plan* that has to change.

AVERY. You've been very forthcoming with us...I wonder if we could prevail upon you...?

TAGGART. What would *I* do?

AVERY. Please.

TAGGART. I would ask myself how much I wanted this.

AVERY. Assume that the importance of this action is beyond measure.

TAGGART. In that case, I would reconsider my priorities.

AVERY. Well. Talk to us.

MAXWELL. Please. It's too much. Gentlemen...

KLING. Please, Kit, don't fuck this up.

AVERY. *(to KLING)* Hey hey hey. What are you doing?

KLING. Oh, come on, Tom. It isn't hard to figure out who we are. Our pictures pop up in the goddamn newspapers, and he already knows *Miles*.

AVERY. I'm not talking about the *names*. I'm talking about your *tone*.

KLING. It's – We're *talking*. We have to know what we're *talking* about.

MAXWELL. I know what we're talking about, / and I resent...

AVERY. Okay. Okay. Look: Let's not fight, or get upset. We're getting what we came here for and now let's, you know, work it through. This is far too important to walk away from. Not before we hear everyone's thoughts. *Kit...?*

KLING. I apologize for my language, Kit.

AVERY. Well, that's – That's fine. So.

Please go on, Mr. Taggart.

TAGGART. Okay. You want to kill a man. You want to cause as little collateral damage as possible. Of course. "As possible" is the key. So the question becomes, how much do you care? What is the cost of each life, compared to the reward of success? It becomes a question

of statistics. Say you're on the battlefield and you just
want to kill one general. If you could pick him off with
a rifle, you *would*, and that would be that. You have
nothing against his soldiers. Everyone goes home. But
you can't get him like that, so you turn to your array of
weapons, and what do you have? Cannons. You can't
hope to kill one man with a cannonball. The idea of a
cannonball is to fire it into a crowd of enemies and see
what it does. It takes this guy's head off, knocks that
guy's arm off, bounces around, breaks another guy's
leg. You don't care *which* guys; it's a weapon of general
destruction. It's addressed to "Occupant." "To whom
it may concern," right? You're working with statistics.
Now somebody figured out that you could improve a
cannonball by filling it with gunpowder and lighting
the fuse before you fire it. *Now* it takes out two or three
guys, then it blows up and kills three more. Now what
if you had enough cannonballs to kill everyone? Or
better yet, one giant cannonball that kills everyone in
one shot. You would get your man, wouldn't you? Your
one man. But before you do it, you have that question:
"Do I want him that bad? Or can I let him live so that
these others may live?"

Folks: This can be done. You just have to want to do it.

AVERY. Are you talking about the whole *building*?

TAGGART. No no. It doesn't have to be *that* crazy.

I'm talking about the whole *room*.

(*pause*)

MAXWELL. You can't get a bomb into that room.

TAGGART. You can get a *missile* in.

(*pause*)

AVERY. A *missile*? Oh, my God.

MAXWELL. Have we heard all we wanted to hear?

AVERY. (*to* **TAGGART**) The people in that room would not
be soldiers.

TAGGART. Would they have nuked Berlin to kill Hitler?

KLING. No question about *that*. They nuked / *Japan*...

TAGGART. So, if you knew what *building* Hitler was in…? Or, better yet, what *room* he was in…?

I'm not telling you what to do. I don't know what your cause is or who the *man* is. *You* have to decide how far you're willing to go. You're just asking me if he can be killed, and I'm telling you *anyone* can be killed if your resources are great enough or you don't have to get away with it or you're willing to die.

AVERY. We would have to get away with it.

KLING. And live, please.

TAGGART. Too bad. Because the best option – even better than the missile – is to put someone in that room who was willing to pay the price.

AVERY. That's better than a *missile?*

TAGGART. *Oh* yeah.

KLING. Yeah, but…

AVERY. The Hitler plotters, the ones that plotted against Hitler, the German, um, *officers…?*

TAGGART. Yeah?

AVERY. They got into the room and it didn't *work.*

TAGGART. Von Stauffenberg was operating at a critical disadvantage: He wanted to live. He thought he could place the package and leave the room. Somebody moved it a few feet and Hitler survived.

KLING. Keitel.

TAGGART. Brandt. If Von Stauffenberg had stayed, he would have seen the job to the end.

AVERY. Well. If we *had* a person who was willing to…sacrifice himself, we couldn't get him into that room. And we couldn't get a weapon in there under *any* circumstances.

TAGGART. Sure you could.

AVERY. We *could?*

TAGGART. There's always a way.

AVERY. *Well.*

Still. I think it would have to be the missile. Can we get a missile?

KLING. That won't be a problem.

AVERY. It *won't?*

KLING. No.

AVERY. My God.

TAGGART. How big is the room?

KLING. Oh, Christ. Thirty by...fifteen, maybe?

TAGGART. You'll want a shoulder-mounted system with a high-explosive warhead. Optically sighted. Heat-seeker disabled. Line-of-sight only. Double whammy charge.

AVERY. Wow.

MAXWELL. Good *Lord*, Tom.

AVERY. About this warhead... You couldn't just...I don't know...*shoot* this man with a missile, so it would kill him but not...not actually, you know...blow *up?*

TAGGART. Like a cannonball?

KLING. Tom...

AVERY. Like a very large bullet. Is that...?

TAGGART. No, it's a good question. You're trying to save people's lives. Because you're good men. But it's a rocket. And rockets tend to keep going until they blow up. Through walls. Floors. Out the other side of the building...

AVERY. I see.

TAGGART. I'm not sure how many lives you would save.

AVERY. Okay.

TAGGART. But it's a good point. Because that's why you want the double whammy. *Bang* through the window, then *big* bang, so it frags the room, and not beyond. It needs to be contained.

MAXWELL. How do you mean, "frags"?

TAGGART. Well, first there's the blast, which is enough right there to peel everyone's face off. Then there's the fragmentation of the missile itself, which is like a million little BBs to shred your flesh. Then you lay there and burn.

MAXWELL. And what would be the possibility for success in such an attack?

TAGGART. Success being the death of this one man.

MAXWELL. Well, of course! You do understand that that's the *point*, don't you? The / *only* point to the whole thing!

TAGGART. Yes. Yes, sir, I do. I'm only clarifying my answer.

MAXWELL. Well, what is it?

TAGGART. I'm guessing about seventy-five percent.

AVERY. Oh.

MAXWELL. *Tom...*

AVERY. I guess – I'm sorry, but I guess I thought it would be higher.

TAGGART. Then I apologize for not making myself clearer. This is a *better* plan. But, uh, to pull off something like this on the first attempt, when it has to be on this particular day in this particular place...It's too restricting. If you don't get him the first time, all I can say is the man can't live forever.

AVERY. No, we haven't made this clear. It's not that we *want* to do it on this day. We / *have* to.

KLING. If he lives 'till April twelfth it's over. We've lost.

AVERY. Jeff...

KLING. It's this one shot. It's this one / shot or it's nothing.

AVERY. Jeff, that's a little specific.

KLING. Tom, we're way past that. He's *in*.

TAGGART. *(to* **KLING***)* Well, now...

KLING. *(to* **TAGGART***)* Listen: There's an incredible amount of money in this for you. If you can appreciate that. An incredible amount of money. I mean – to be crude. Now let's *fix* this.

TAGGART. Then put someone in the room.

AVERY. Let's talk about that.

KLING. If the missile is big enough, you can blow up the whole goddamn *floor.*
I'm sorry. I know it hurts but come *on.* Are we gonna get serious about this or not? Like the man says, how bad do we want it? I mean – ...?

AVERY. All right, Jeff.

KLING. *Fine.*

TAGGART. Maybe this is the test of your idealology, right? "Will someone *die* for this?"

AVERY. I cannot stress strongly enough how extreme will be the level of security at this meeting. If we found someone, he would have to get *in.*

MAXWELL. *I* can get in.

(pause)

AVERY. What are you saying?

MAXWELL. I'm saying I can get into that meeting. I can get in there and I can kill the son of a bitch. And you fellows can kiss my ass.

AVERY. You're confusing me, Kit.

MAXWELL. *(to* **TAGGART***)* If you say it can be done, tell me how to do it.

AVERY. Kit, are you trying to be *funny?*

MAXWELL. Yes, Tom. It's my famous sense of humor. Now let's talk about this.

KLING. No, no. It's no good. Thank you, Kit, but no.

MAXWELL. What are our chances if *I* do it?

TAGGART. Well. That would depend upon *you,* sir. Are you…? I'm sorry, but are you *up* to it?

KLING. No, Kit. You're not *up* to it. I'm sorry, but this is too important. Everything is / riding on this.

AVERY. It's true, Kit. Everything, yes, everything is riding on this.

MAXWELL. Not if we do both.

AVERY. How do you mean?

MAXWELL. I can do my part. I can make sure he stays in the room. Stays in his seat. And when the time comes, I can shoot him. Kill him. And just to make sure – just in case something goes wrong – there's the other thing.

AVERY. What other thing?

MAXWELL. The rocket. The missile. The other thing. It happens at the same time. What does *that* do for our statistics?

KLING. You want to – ? I just want to understand this. You want to go in there and kill him, and we *still* fire the missile? You *still* want us to go ahead and kill everyone in the room?

MAXWELL. I don't see any other way. Do you? Now, that would have to put us up near a hundred percent. Right?

AVERY. You're proposing *suicide*. Kit, do you want to *die?*

MAXWELL. We were talking about commitment. Well, I'm committed.

AVERY. But it doesn't make sense. The whole idea…

MAXWELL. Is what? What are *you* in it for?

AVERY. I thought we…Well, we want to, we want to…Not that it's everything, but we want to *reap*…the rewards… of our work. Don't we?

MAXWELL. My reward is that the son of a bitch dies and goes to hell. Whatever you – and Jeff – get from it, well, good for you.

(*pause*)

TAGGART. So we're working on *both* plans.

MAXWELL. We're doing two plans. At the same time. So that everyone dies. It's decided. *Now* what?

AVERY. The loss of *life*. It couldn't be more important, of course, but every person in the *room*? These are innocent people, for heaven's sake. Some of them are our *friends*. It was one thing to talk about a man who… Well, this is an enemy to all we hold dear. This man is trying to / undermine our…

MAXWELL. Tom, what is it you want? You want us to talk you into it? I just laid down my life for this. The more you try to impress us with your perspective, the more likely I am to change my mind. So wrap it up.

AVERY. All right, Kit. But I'm not – I resent – Oh, for goodness' sake, I just think we shouldn't proceed without acknowledging that these people, well…that the *sacrifice* we're / making here…

MAXWELL. Listen to me. If *I'm* going to die, *they* are going to die. I am not going to destroy myself for a fair-to-*good* chance of success. That's the package I'm offering. If you really want to save everyone's life, just say so right now and we'll all go home and await our fate.

KLING. I would have to offer an obvious objection to *that* scenario, no offense / to anyone.

AVERY. Please. Indulge me for a moment, and then I promise to surrender to the inevitable. All I am saying… is that we must…What we must never lose sight of… is the enormous gravity of what we are doing here. If innocent people must die for the greater good, well, that's the burden we choose to bear. But we will never, ever bear it lightly.

TAGGART. The history of the world is the story of good men making hard choices.

AVERY. Yes. Thank you. And we'll keep that in mind always.

TAGGART. All right. Okay. Okay, then.

AVERY. Good powwow.

TAGGART. *(to* **KLING***)* You said something about an incredible amount of money.

End of Scene

Scene Two

*(*MAXWELL *and* FLETCHER. *Maxwell's office.)*

MAXWELL. I understand "compromise." And I'll tell you how it begins: It begins with a man who wants to know what you believe in. Do you believe in The Law? In "Hell"…?

FLETCHER. Um…

MAXWELL. Hm?

FLETCHER. I…Is that rhetorical?

MAXWELL. No, no. I mean, Yes, if it makes you uncomfortable. / I'm just…

FLETCHER. I'm sorry. I'm just concerned about your time. / I have –

MAXWELL. I'm fine. I have no / appointments…

FLETCHER. I know you must be busy, or – that you value / your time…

MAXWELL. I'm fine. / Are you…

FLETCHER. I have this – I'm sorry.

MAXWELL. No, go on. But don't you want a drink?

FLETCHER. No, thank you, really. I just don't know how much time you have to give me and it would be awful if I didn't get around to this Compromise Agreement.

MAXWELL. *Proposed* Compromise Agreement.

FLETCHER. Of course.

MAXWELL. Well, I assume you're going to *leave* it with me, Alex, right?

FLETCHER. If you don't mind. / And…

MAXWELL. Well…

FLETCHER. I'm sorry, and it's *Allan*, actually.

MAXWELL. Oh, Christ. I apologize…

FLETCHER. No, it's okay.

MAXWELL. I'm getting old, I guess.

FLETCHER. Not at all. / A man of your…

MAXWELL. But *Allan*. You're going to *leave* me the Compromise, are you not? You're not going to ask me to read it *now*, are you? What have you got there, three hundred pages?

FLETCHER. Four hundred and ten, sir. / And this...

MAXWELL. Ah *hah*.

FLETCHER. And this is just the summary, of course. Yeah. But I was hoping we could *discuss* it, / just to...

MAXWELL. Sort of summarize the summary, you mean?

FLETCHER. Kind of. Just to make my best case, smooth some of the / edges...

MAXWELL. Your best case is in the *summary*, I hope.

FLETCHER. Sure. / But...

MAXWELL. Then we'll meet again. *After* I've read it.

FLETCHER. That's fair enough, Mr. Maxwell. I just can't overemphasize how important I think this is. I really think I have the best possible deal for everyone involved. / The n– The...

MAXWELL. Not for our side.

FLETCHER. Hm. Mr. Maxwell, I really think / you'll fi–

MAXWELL. The best deal for *us* is no compromise at all.

FLETCHER. This is the best *possible* deal, sir. It's time for us to be realistic. We're about to lose everything. The only course of action is to see what we can save. / And th–

MAXWELL. To beg.

FLETCHER. I'm sorry?

MAXWELL. To beg. Before a despicable man. A man whom I – and a great many others – despise. What about you? Do you like him?

FLETCHER. Mr. Maxwell, I'm sorry, but that is as far from the point as it can be / right now.

MAXWELL. I don't think / so.

FLETCHER. And this is not begging. It's a mutually – a mutually...

MAXWELL. I'll read it. / Okay?

FLETCHER. ...beneficial...

MAXWELL. I'll read it.

FLETCHER. Thank you, sir. Really. Thank you. But if I could just have *five* minutes...

MAXWELL. You can have more than that, Allan. And a drink, too. Please.

FLETCHER. Any soft drink would be fine. Thank you.

MAXWELL. A *soft* drink, Allan. What are you afraid of?

FLETCHER. Nothing, sir. I'm just – Well, I'm afraid of a *drink*, actually. I've had a problem with that, before.

MAXWELL. You've – Well, hell, I'm sorry about that. I'm being very rude.

FLETCHER. No. / Please.

MAXWELL. No, I'm sorry, / I should mind my own business.

FLETCHER. Please. No. It's nothing.

MAXWELL. Well. More ice?

FLETCHER. No. That's great. Thank you.

MAXWELL. I'll read this thing, Allan.

FLETCHER. Thank you, Mr. Maxwell. I've gone over every clause, / every possible...

MAXWELL. I'm sure you have. I'm just trying to get to know the man who wrote it. That's important, too, don't you think?

FLETCHER. With all due respect, sir, I don't. This Compromise is more important than I am. The first / priority...

MAXWELL. Jefferson didn't *mail* in his work, did he? He had to back it up with the force of his character.

FLETCHER. Mr. Maxwell, Jefferson's character was a lot flimsier than his work.

MAXWELL. I've noticed that I'm calling you "Allan" and you're calling me "Mr. Maxwell."

FLETCHER. I guess I thought you preferred it that way.

MAXWELL. My mistake, then. And I'm sorry you thought that. I miss the old formalities. I do. But I had to give up the battle long ago. People introduce me by my first name to their children. To their young *children*. I'll tell you what: You may call me Kit if you like, but I think I'll call you "Mr. Fletcher."

FLETCHER. Then I'll continue to call you "Mr. Maxwell."

MAXWELL. Fine. It'll be our secret code that mystifies the world. Mr. Fletcher: I was telling you how it begins.

FLETCHER. Yes, sir. But you were talking about a different kind of compromise.

MAXWELL. Are you so sure?

FLETCHER. This Compromise is not a moral one.

MAXWELL. It isn't "moral," huh?

FLETCHER. It isn't – Ha. No, I mean it isn't a "moral / compromise."

MAXWELL. I know. I know. Who else is on board?

FLETCHER. My office. In spirit, I mean. No one has read this draft yet.

MAXWELL. But you've been selling it for…?

FLETCHER. Months. Many months.

MAXWELL. To no avail.

FLETCHER. We have the endorsement of literally thousands of / prominent…

MAXWELL. Sure, sure. But not from the people who count. Not from the people who will actually, in fact, compromise.

FLETCHER. Mr. Maxwell, they're all waiting for someone like you.

MAXWELL. What's wrong with someone like *you*?

FLETCHER. I guess I'm not a great salesman.

MAXWELL. A good product sells itself.

FLETCHER. With all due respect, sir, I have found that not to be the case.

MAXWELL. Maybe not. What do I know? I've never thought of myself as much of a salesman either.

FLETCHER. Now you're being too modest.

MAXWELL. Am I? That's not necessarily flattery. I knew a great salesman once. His family name was Beneš. B-E-N-E-Š. He was descended from a Magyar conqueror. But you know how he pronounced it?

FLETCHER. No.

MAXWELL. "Beans." Easier for his customers to remember. So he called himself "Beans." Taught his sons to call themselves "Beans." Turned his family name into something absurd. Something funny. To sell paint. To be a "great salesman."

FLETCHER. You're too hard on him. I'm sure he found pride in his shrewdness.

MAXWELL. Really? Would you have let me keep calling you Alex if it meant I would endorse your Compromise?

FLETCHER. Absolutely.

MAXWELL. Forever?

FLETCHER. You can call me whatever you want. *Especially* if you endorse the Compromise.

MAXWELL. What if I told you to change it for the world? Never be Allan Fletcher again?

FLETCHER. Are you?

MAXWELL. Am I what?

FLETCHER. I don't know. Are we approaching some sort of agreement here?

MAXWELL. What? No, goddammit. What could that even mean? / I'm trying...

FLETCHER. Sorry.

MAXWELL. I'm trying to...plumb your...psyche.

FLETCHER. I'm sorry. I was prepared to / gauge the offer.

MAXWELL. I'm not as subtle as you think I am.

FLETCHER. No offense intended.

MAXWELL. Did you think I wanted to put my name...

FLETCHER. I honestly am not / assuming anything...

MAXWELL. ...On your Proposal?

FLETCHER. No. I make no assumptions. I recognize the efficacy of anything.

MAXWELL. You recognize the efficacy of anything, do you?

FLETCHER. I do.

MAXWELL. But you don't refrain from making moral judgments.

FLETCHER. I do not.

MAXWELL. You have opinions.

FLETCHER. I do.

MAXWELL. *(re: the document)* As expressed within?

FLETCHER. Not at all.

MAXWELL. Your opinions are not expressed within the corners of this document?

FLETCHER. No, sir.

MAXWELL. What is, then?

FLETCHER. Efficacy.

MAXWELL. I see. But you have judgments and opinions.

FLETCHER. Of course.

MAXWELL. Are you judgmental and opinionated?

FLETCHER. I hope not. But, alas…

MAXWELL. Of course you are. You didn't get where you are…

But what does it feel like to be so opinionated and yet powerless?

FLETCHER. I'm not sure I'm either of those things / entirely.

MAXWELL. Oh, come on. I'm not trying to offend you. But I'll bet you're not always so polite; you couldn't be. I'll bet a lot of people wish you'd just shut up and go away. Sometimes, right?

FLETCHER. Probably.

MAXWELL. And you're terribly successful, compared to the average person, but it's all relative, right? You're at the mercy of the very powerful. And, for some reason that I hope to have explained to me, the very powerful are always, always fools.

FLETCHER. Present company excepted, of course.

MAXWELL. I should goddamn well hope so.

Present company may have had too much to drink. I'm not trying to...

FLETCHER. It's okay.

MAXWELL. I just don't know how you do it.

FLETCHER. One day at a time, as they say.

MAXWELL. Oh, Christ, I'm not talking about the drinking.

FLETCHER. No, I knew you weren't. I didn't / mean to suggest...

MAXWELL. I'm talking about how you can keep trying to sell sense to the insensible.

FLETCHER. Well, sir...

MAXWELL. From *your* point of view, that is. I'm not suggesting that I think your ideas are right. In fact, I might as well just say, as I'm positive it will be no surprise to you, that I think you're wrong. That you're dead wrong and you might be dangerous.

FLETCHER. I guess that's no surprise.

MAXWELL. ...That you might be a goddamned danger to us all.

FLETCHER. I really hope that I can convince you / otherwise.

MAXWELL. ...But then the very powerful are always fools. And I am *dreadfully* powerful.

FLETCHER. Ha ha. Well, I do admire the complexity of your thinking. *(re: the Compromise)* Which is why...

MAXWELL. I've seen you around, you know. I remember now. I've seen you on TV.

FLETCHER. Oh. I'm just glad I'm on your radar.

MAXWELL. Yeah. As I recall, you have a tendency to look astonished when people don't agree with you.

FLETCHER. Huh. That's probably a tactic, as much as anything.

MAXWELL. Oh, come on. It's no tactic. It's as if you really can't figure out why people aren't fired up by your message of, what? Of "empathy"? "Logic"?

FLETCHER. Hm. I told you: I need a salesman.

MAXWELL. You need a product. You're defeated, Mr. Fletcher, I have to say, because your ideas are…I don't want to say "dull." Unattractive. They lack…

FLETCHER. Anger?

MAXWELL. *Atavism.* They lack *atavism.* You know what that means?

FLETCHER. Something primal, I guess, right? But that doesn't say much for people.

MAXWELL. It just says we're people, that's all.
But you don't need me to tell you. You've thought about it, surely. Come clean.

FLETCHER. I've thought about it.

MAXWELL. So you know what I'm saying.

FLETCHER. I'm in my car the other day, in a long line at a traffic light. And the car at the front of the line runs the red light. After a second, the next car runs the light. And a few seconds later, the *next* car. Obviously, the other guys only did it because the first guy did it. They received *inspiration.* I have to work so hard…*(re: the document)*…at this. But a guy runs a red light and they're *inspired.*

MAXWELL. Of course. A good product sells itself.

(He laughs.)

FLETCHER. So I know what you're talking about. But I'm not defeated.

MAXWELL. Trust me, Mr. Fletcher. You're defeated.

FLETCHER. I'm in the door.

MAXWELL. But I'm intractable.

FLETCHER. Then why are you indulging me?

MAXWELL. You never know. We need a solution. Yours is no good, but you might come up with a better one. You might say just the right thing. I've heard a lot of talk about open-mindedness; I thought I'd try it.

FLETCHER. How do you like it?

MAXWELL. I don't care for it. You might be defeated.

FLETCHER. I don't think so.

MAXWELL. Do you want another dr– *soft* drink?

FLETCHER. Just water. If you're sure you have *time* for me.

MAXWELL. I said I did. Why? Am I pushing you too hard?

FLETCHER. Of course not. I was just / hoping…

MAXWELL. Delving into your…existential crisis?

FLETCHER. Is that what it's called?

MAXWELL. Hell, I don't know. I hear people say "existential crisis." I'm not sure what that means.

FLETCHER. Me neither.

MAXWELL. I don't mean to be hard on you. / I know –

FLETCHER. No, not at –

MAXWELL. Hm?

FLETCHER. Not at all.

MAXWELL. It's because you've been on the same road too long. Your crisis. I understand your despair. I know what it is to stick with something. There's a…*fear*… of…

FLETCHER. Hm.

MAXWELL. What?

FLETCHER. A fear of…?

MAXWELL. Not "fear." Nobility.

FLETCHER. Oh.

MAXWELL. Yeah. Nobility. Taking your…convictions…to the grave, if you will.

FLETCHER. Unchanging, you mean.

MAXWELL. Resolute. Is a better word.

FLETCHER. Well…

MAXWELL. Well, what?

FLETCHER. You said fear.

MAXWELL. That isn't what I meant. I corrected myself. Because you're trying to suggest "fear of change." Right?

FLETCHER. Yes.

MAXWELL. Well…But the weakness, the weakness that you're implying, could be in the *changing*. Not in the *refusal* to change. See?

FLETCHER. We're all supposed to change. Otherwise we'd still be infants.

MAXWELL. No, you're not following me: the point is am I changing because I'm *illuminated*? "Ah ha, I see it now." Or am I changing because I'm afraid of…of *sacrifice*? See?

I'll tell you s– It's funny we're having this…this conversation. I had a dream just last night. I was in some exotic land. It's dusk. Twilight. I've done a lot of travelling, as you can guess, and I've noticed that you never feel so far from home in a foreign land, as when the sun is setting. "Oh, Christ, he's gonna tell me his dreams."

FLETCHER. No. Ha ha. No. I'm honored. Hm.

MAXWELL. Right. So. You know. So it's twilight in this place, and these little foreign men were leading me to the *chopping block*. To cut my *head* off. I tell you, it was completely real for me. I honestly *believed* these little foreign bastards were gonna cut my head off. I was actually contemplating my last moments. How I should go out, you know? And of course it was very important to me that I go out with dignity and courage. And and and…there were others being beheaded too, and as I watched them in…in abject horror, I – as scared as I was, I spent this time planning how I would stand – straight and tall, and how I would make a brief but wise speech, and there would be this calm smile on my face as the axe fell. Right?

FLETCHER. Yeah.

MAXWELL. And, as scared as I was – because this dream was extremely real, as I said – I was proud of myself, because I knew I would die well. And then, at the very last second, as they led me forward to the block, this thought came to me with the simplicity of perfect logic…?

FLETCHER. Okay.

MAXWELL. At the very last second I said to myself: "Hey. I could *run*." As if this was a brand new concept that was in no way contradictory to my previous plan! "I could *run*." Like, Hey, why didn't I think of that *before*! So I ran. After all that planning, I just made a run for it. And as I was running around – and, by the way, I haven't *run*, waking or sleeping, for thirty years – as I was running from these scary little foreign bastards, I thought, "You *idiot*. You *coward*. You blew it."

FLETCHER. Well.

MAXWELL. Yeah. You see what I'm saying?

FLETCHER. I wouldn't take it too seriously.

MAXWELL. I…Well, I *don't* take it seriously. It's just an example of, uh…

FLETCHER. Mm.

MAXWELL. It's an *analogy*. Like your traffic-light thing. To / *show* you…

FLETCHER. Right. Of course.

MAXWELL. So…But why wouldn't you take it seriously?

FLETCHER. I don't put a lot of stock in dreams.

MAXWELL. You don't think dreams mean anything?

FLETCHER. Why try to learn from the confusion of dreams when our waking lives tell us all we need to know?

MAXWELL. "Why try to –" By God, Fletcher, you must have been one hell of a companionable drunk. Almost a shame. Anyway, thank you for that.

FLETCHER. Not at all.

MAXWELL. But let me ask you something. Do you remember the house of your early childhood?

FLETCHER. Sure.

MAXWELL. And how long has it been since you lived there?

FLETCHER. Twenty years.

MAXWELL. And how often do you think of it?

FLETCHER. Rarely.

MAXWELL. But how often do you dream of it?

You see? Too often, to mean nothing. Too often, for the dream to mean nothing.

You don't concede my point?

FLETCHER. Very interesting.

MAXWELL. You're sulking, a little bit.

FLETCHER. Not at all. I'm / just thi– ...think–

MAXWELL. A little bit, I think. You don't like being challenged. Or just not by me, maybe.

FLETCHER. Nothing could be / farther from the...

MAXWELL. Or, you know what? You don't like not having thought of everything. I'll bet you never say "I never thought of that."

It's okay. Don't be offended. I like to find where a person's ego lives. Usually it's too easy. You should be flattered that you're interesting.

FLETCHER. Thank you. I am. Flattered. But, sir. People are dying. There are people / whose lives depend upon... depend...

MAXWELL. Don't tell me about the dying people, Mr. Fletcher. That's not the conversation we're having today.

FLETCHER. We have the opportunity / to do something...

MAXWELL. We're not – Look. What we do, Mr. Fletcher. What we do...is what our fathers tell us.

FLETCHER. I don't understand what you mean.

MAXWELL. It's true nevertheless, though. Huh? Nevertheless.

Or were you an *angry* drunk?

FLETCHER. What do you mean?

MAXWELL. I speculated that you were a companionable drunk, but now I wonder if you weren't an angry one.

FLETCHER. Uh...

MAXWELL. You don't remember? You don't have to say.

FLETCHER. I guess I was a *complicated* drunk.

MAXWELL. Uh oh. I wonder what that means. It can't be good.

FLETCHER. Well…

MAXWELL. I don't know if he was descended from a Magyar conqueror. I just made that part up.

FLETCHER. Well, sir. If you'd rather not discuss this today…?

MAXWELL. No no no. I understand. That's fine. Don't leave it like that. Let's give a minute or two to the…to the Proposal…What have we here…? Just let me… Did you want a cup of coffee, or something?

FLETCHER. No, thank you. If you do want to discuss it, well, the most – "controversial," I guess – the most controversial clause is summarized… Oh, where's / my copy?

MAXWELL. I can't abide this man. I cannot *abide* him.

FLETCHER. Mr. Maxwell. Once and for all. Pardon me. But sir… We have got to get beyond / this rigid, I would say *dangerous,* sir, *dangerous…*

MAXWELL. Oh, yes. Yes. I know what you're going to say. That's fine for *you,* just fine. I know. But this is war. A kind of war. And you're standing at the gates of the fortress saying "Just open it up. Just a little." But if you turned around you'd see that there's a…that there's an *army* behind you!

FLETCHER. Sir…

MAXWELL. If that kind of talk makes you nervous, I'm sorry, but you'll *ruin* us eventually and you'll be glad to see us go. You'll be glad, but what about *us*?!
    You'd see us all hanging from the lampposts before you're done.

FLETCHER. Mr. Maxwell. I will be sitting at that table with or without your support. Now, you can sit there and play the martyr, watch everything you fought for slip away. Or you can stand up next to me and and say this is fair. This is justice. Now, I'm sorry about this, but you're either going to / hear it from me now…

MAXWELL. Wait a minute. Hold on a minute.

FLETCHER. …Hear it from me now or hear it from me / in that room.

MAXWELL. Wait a minute.

FLETCHER. …Hear it from me before the world. As it were.

MAXWELL. What table?

FLETCHER. You have a chance to make a different kind of history / here, sir…

MAXWELL. What table? / What room?

FLETCHER. Please. I'm sorry. Please just read the Proposal, and promise to meet with me again. I spoke out of turn; I'm sorry.

MAXWELL. Yes, but what table?

FLETCHER. In the room. The meeting.

(pause)

MAXWELL. You'll be at the meeting.

FLETCHER. Yes, sir. I thought you understood that.

MAXWELL. They gave you a chair at the meeting.

FLETCHER. I hope you don't have a problem with that. Perhaps I'm being taken more seriously than you thought.

MAXWELL. Maybe so.

FLETCHER. All the more reason to get on board.

MAXWELL. Hm.

FLETCHER. I'm sorry about that. That was glib.

MAXWELL. Hm?

FLETCHER. I was rude.

MAXWELL. No, that's…

FLETCHER. I should have said that I need your help.

MAXWELL. Yeah. Well, sir. Allan. Mr. Fletcher. I can't change. I have to be "resolute."

FLETCHER. If you could just read it. Tell me what you think. If you / could just –

MAXWELL. There are things you can't talk me into.

FLETCHER. Could just…If you could just listen to me…

MAXWELL. No.

No.

You've wasted your time.

End of Scene

Scene Three

(**AVERY** *and* **KLING**)

KLING. And all that stuff about cannonballs. What the heck was that?

AVERY. Well – heh – He was trying to create a context for us, I think, so we could see… / ah…

KLING. Sure, sure, but, / uh…

AVERY. I know, though. Heh. I was wondering myself. Heh heh. But, you know, you've got to appreciate: *He's* nervous *too.*

KLING. Well, sure.

AVERY. It's an unusual situation for everyone. I *hope.* / I *hope* it's…

KLING. I would hope so, yeah.

AVERY. So everyone is gonna be a little, *you* know…

KLING. I know. But still…

AVERY. It was a big interview for him.

KLING. Oh, I'm sure.

AVERY. Yeah, you know it was. He's fine.

KLING. Hm. He'd better be.

AVERY. No, I'm sure he is. He seems like a good man.

KLING. Well…I hope he appreciates how much is at stake.

AVERY. Did you talk to Miles again?

KLING. I can't reach him. I don't know where he is.

AVERY. Really?

KLING. That's not unusual.

AVERY. It concerns me a bit.

KLING. No, no. He eats our bread.

AVERY. What?

KLING. He sings our song.

AVERY. I don't know that / figure of…

KLING. He's fine. Don't worry. He needs to stay underground.

AVERY. Wow. It's very exciting. Kind of scary, huh?

KLING. Tom. There's no reason / to get…

AVERY. No no. I know. I'm just saying, these shadowy doings...

KLING. Kind of a thrill, huh?

AVERY. Well, I don't want to seem callous, but...I'm only human.

KLING. Sure. It's *exciting.*

AVERY. It's hard to concentrate on anything else these days. But that's between you and me, / obviously.

KLING. Oh, I know. I know. I wouldn't...Well, I wouldn't expect Kit to understand, if you know / what I mean.

AVERY. Unh uh. I should say not. That's a terrible shame, don't get me wrong.

KLING. Yeah.

AVERY. It's mind-boggling, really. What he's doing. I can't say I completely understand it.

KLING. Really?

AVERY. Why?

KLING. Well, I'm not questioning his dedication, by any means. He's always been one of the hard-liners. From *way* back. But. I think he must also be a little, you know, weary of life. You would have to be. I think.

AVERY. Yes, but all those *other people.* I find his attitude about that to be a little surprising.

KLING. I guess I really don't.

AVERY. You don't?

KLING. He's thinking about his legacy.

AVERY. How do you mean?

KLING. He doesn't want to go down in the books as an assassin.

AVERY. I don't get it.

KLING. No witnesses. He doesn't want any living witnesses. This way, he's just one of the dead.

AVERY. You're kidding me.

KLING. You find that surprising?

AVERY. You're telling me that he's willing to kill, he's willing to die, and yet he's frightened of being *found out?*

KLING. If you ask me, that's Kit Maxwell all over.

AVERY. That's an odd theory, Kling.

KLING. He pretends to be disgusted with us, but *he'll* kill *anyone*. He's so enamored of his legacy he'll kill anyone to protect it. His dignity. He'd kill you if you caught him picking his *nose*.

AVERY. He pretends to be disgusted with us?

KLING. Yeah.

AVERY. He's disgusted with us?

KLING. He pretends to be.

AVERY. He pretends to be *disgusted* with us?

KLING. Well, yeah.

AVERY. *(hurt)* I didn't get that.

KLING. Anyway.

AVERY. Well, it's not to take away from his sacrifice.

KLING. No.

AVERY. These deaths are on all our heads.

KLING. Yeah. But if you went back to the sniper plan, he'd be out.

AVERY. He's made that clear.

KLING. Don't I know it.

AVERY. It puts me in mind of the ancient Athenians.

KLING. Yeah, me too.

AVERY. Really?

KLING. No. Of course not.

AVERY. Oh. Well, their entire culture was based on the avoidance of shame. Not *guilt*, mind you. Never *guilt*. But *shame*.

KLING. You mean, like every *other* entire culture?

AVERY. Hm?

KLING. Tom, you're describing *everyone*. Forget the Athenians.

AVERY. No no. I'm saying...

KLING. Sure. They're totally unique in that respect. Point taken.

AVERY. It's a terrible thing to have to kill all those people.

KLING. Our hands are tied.

AVERY. I know, but some of them are good people. Many of them are quite sympathetic to our cause.

KLING. We'll have to think of them as martyrs.

AVERY. Of course.

   (pause)

KLING. But, you know…

AVERY. What.

KLING. I just have to say, you know – and I know, I know – but I just won't miss that bastard Hetzinger, / from…

AVERY. Oh yes.

KLING. From the Secretary's / Office.

AVERY. No doubt.

KLING. And that bitch from…What the hell country is she from?

AVERY. Hm.

KLING. God, I hope she's flammable, that one.

AVERY. I'm sure sh– Well, we'll see.

   (A buzzer sounds.)

KLING. Which one is this?

   *(**AVERY** presses a hidden button. **MAXWELL** enters.)*

MAXWELL. Tom. Jeff.

AVERY. Good to see you, Kit. *(He goes to hug him.)*

MAXWELL. Oh, Tom. Please.

AVERY. All right. But I'm glad to see you.

MAXWELL. I'm sorry I'm late. I've been putting my affairs in order, as they say.

AVERY. It's okay. Tag's not here yet, anyway.

KLING. You're putting your affairs in order?

MAXWELL. As they say.

KLING. Kit, you can't be putting your affairs in order.

MAXWELL. I can't?

KLING. What if someone notices? You can't be seen putting your affairs in order. It's kind of a giveaway, isn't it? "Hey, what's with Maxwell? He's putting all his affairs in order. What's *he* planning?"

MAXWELL. I've been very discreet.

KLING. I'm sure you have, Kit, but still: You never know what's gonna catch someone's eye.

MAXWELL. You mean, like the recent purchase of a *missile?*

KLING. Some things are necessary and some things aren't. We shouldn't do anything more than necessary.

MAXWELL. It is *necessary* to put my affairs in *order.*

KLING. I'm not trying to be – Look, the whole Watergate thing was about a piece of *tape* left on a *door.*

MAXWELL. Huh? What the hell are you talking about, Jeff?

KLING. I'm sorry, but I think I'm making sense here. *We're* not going into that room. *You* are. Those guys are – right now – digging up everything they can find on everyone who's gonna walk through that door. Like, "Now, has anyone been putting their *affairs* in *order?*" for example. I'm just – Tom?

MAXWELL. All right. Forget it. I'll stop putting my affairs in order. Sorry.

KLING. *I'm* sorry.

AVERY. That said, Kit, I want you to know I'm just as impressed as I can be with you. You're a true hero.

MAXWELL. Thank you.

AVERY. Yes. Yes. I feel that I need to tell you something about myself. I hope you'll understand this.

(The buzzer sounds.)

Well. Another time.

(He presses the button and **TAGGART** *enters, carrying a briefcase.)*

TAGGART. Gentlemen, / it's good to see you.

AVERY. Tag, / how are you?

KLING. Tag.

TAGGART. I've just been finishing this up, and I think you'll like it.

AVERY. Do you want a drink or something?

TAGGART. No thanks. Maybe in a bit.

So. A briefcase. Mr. Maxwell, you'll want to be front row center for this...

A briefcase. During the meeting, your watch will beep about, let's say, ten seconds before the designated moment, at which time you'll reach for your

briefcase…? As if to get some papers or something…?
Some documentation? Uh, some *form* or something…?
A visual / *aid…*?

MAXWELL. *Yes.* I can *imagine.*

TAGGART. Yes. And as you grasp the handle and pull back this flap…

(*He whips out the handle, which has a knife attached.*)

Straight for the jugular – which is right here – as many times as you can before the…impact. The missile. And that should make him as dead as you could ever want him.

AVERY. Wow. That is first-class work, Tag.

KLING. What is it made of?

TAGGART. Fiberglass. The metal detectors won't freak out.

KLING. What about the X-ray machines?

TAGGART. The knife sits inside the same rectangular piece that it was cut from. Perfect fit. No seams. So the machine just sees a rectangle that looks like the mounting for the handle. In fact, it *is* the mounting for the handle.

AVERY. Man, that's something.

KLING. May I?

TAGGART. Sure. But be careful. We don't want to ruin the fit.

(**KLING** *sheathes the knife into the briefcase.*)

AVERY. Do you have a *workshop,* / of some…?

TAGGART. My buddy has keys to a place with a / lot of cool tools…

KLING. The handle doesn't fold.

TAGGART. Huh?

KLING. The handle doesn't *fold.*

TAGGART. No, it has to be rigid if you want to hold the knife properly.

KLING. But Tag…

TAGGART. What.

KLING. The handle doesn't *fold.* It doesn't *lay down.*

TAGGART. It looks perfectly normal when you're carrying it.

KLING. But it doesn't look perfectly normal when you're *presenting* it for *inspection.* The handle just sticks up in a rigid...rigid way. "Here is my briefcase, which is indistinguishable from any other, except for the *handle,* which is doing something that no other briefcase has ever done before."

TAGGART. I'm telling you, I already *tried* a folding handle, and you can't control the knife.

KLING. I understand that. We're *beyond* that. That's why it's called a *dilemma.* But now we have this locked-up handle that says, "*Fold* me. I *dare* you. What's *wrong* with me? Have a closer look. Go ahead. No, not *there!* Not under this cheaply-constructed *flap!*"

TAGGART. Okay. Let's roll it back a little, alright? I get it.

AVERY. Tag: I think the handle should be made to fold.

TAGGART. Okay. I'll work on it. It's a *prototype,* okay? But, you know, Jeff, you're not creating a very nurturing environment.

AVERY. Maybe there should be a brass pin or something that could be inserted to make it lock.

TAGGART. Yeah. That's actually what I was thinking. That's *constructive.* Thank you.

AVERY. You're welcome. Did you guys get a chance to see the sniper's nest?

TAGGART. Yeah, we did. There are some issues there.

AVERY. Okay.

TAGGART. For one thing, we have another window to deal with.

AVERY. Oh.

TAGGART. Yeah. Now we can cut a hole in that window, but it's hard to do without attracting attention.

AVERY. Oh. I imagined you would just – bang right through it. With the rocket, you know?

TAGGART. Again...We would be affecting the trajectory at its earliest stage.

KLING. You know, "optically-sighted" and "line-of-sight" are the same thing.

TAGGART. Yeah. So?

KLING. You said "optically-sighted" and "line-of-sight."
They're the same thing.

TAGGART. I didn't s– No, they're not.

KLING. They are.

TAGGART. They're not. They're different. It doesn't matter.

KLING. Of course it matters.

TAGGART. It doesn't… This is childish. Tom, let's / move on.

KLING. Childish? We're *relying* / on you…

AVERY. Yes. *Please,* Jeff. We have a rocket that everyone is
happy with. Is everyone happy with the rocket?
So, that's fine. Now, we were talking about this window,
Jeff.

MAXWELL. Can we back up for a moment, please?

AVERY. Of course.

MAXWELL. Now, I'm sorry about this, but…I thought I
would be given a *gun.* I realize now that no one actually *said* it would be a gun, but it just didn't occur to
me that it would be otherwise.

TAGGART. There's no chance of getting a gun / in there.

KLING. A gun is / impossible, Kit.

MAXWELL. I see that now. I see that. When you said you
could get a weapon in there, I was hearing *gun,* and
you / were thinking…

KLING. You can't have a *gun.*

TAGGART. There's no way we could get a gun / in there.

MAXWELL. All right. Stop *saying* that, for chrissake. I *get* it.
I'm trying to arrive at a point, here.

KLING. What's the problem?

MAXWELL. The problem is, I don't know that I can stab
somebody. I was pretty sure I could *shoot* somebody,
but a *knife…*To actually rip into a person with a knife…
I've never harmed a person in my life. Not physically.
I haven't been in a fistfight since I was nine years old.
And now you're saying take this *knife…*and tear into a
man's *throat* with it…

TAGGART. Just his jugular.

MAXWELL. I have to admit I'm just…squeamish. That's

the only word for it. I'm reconciled with the act itself. But...Well, I'm just afraid of the *gore*.

(pause)

TAGGART. Have you ever cleaned a chicken?

MAXWELL. No.

TAGGART. Oh. Well, you know what you should do, is get a whole bunch of live chickens, or some rabbits – even better – take 'em out to the country... If you just dive in, go at it, I'll bet you'll be surprised how easy it is.

AVERY. Do you think that will help you, Kit? What Tag's saying?

KLING. You know, Kit...I don't want to sound insensitive... But I would be remiss if I didn't point out a certain objective fact of the situation, which is...no matter how bad it is, it's all over in ten seconds. I mean, you can take *anything* for ten seconds, can't you?

MAXWELL. Hm. Is that supposed to make me feel better? The certain knowledge that the very last seconds of my life will be spent in some *chaos* of dreadful carnage? That the last thing I see on this earth will be the spraying blood and torn flesh of another man?

KLING. Of your enemy, Kit. Your / *enemy*.

AVERY. Jeff, I'm not sure you're helping.

KLING. It's how any warrior would want to go out. Think of the *Vikings*.

AVERY. *(to KLING)* Seriously.

KLING. You're a warrior, Kit, whether you know it or not. You always have been. We *all* are, but you're one of the great warriors of the modern age. This is your destiny. This is your chance to make it *literal*. What we have lost, you will give back to us. You will return to us the gift of *ferocity*. And I promise you, we won't let you down.

AVERY. Maybe you should think about that rabbit business, Kit.

MAXWELL. All right. Stop it. I'm sorry I brought it up. I will *inure* myself, if it will shut you up. This is something I can do. I just had a moment, but it's over. I'll do whatever it takes.

TAGGART. That's commensurate, man. Commensurate.

KLING. What?

TAGGART. Commensurate.

MAXWELL. With…?

TAGGART. Hm?

AVERY. Okay. Well. Crisis averted. You're a great man, Kit, that's what I've been wanting to say to you. Jeff is right. You're / doing…

MAXWELL. Okay, Tom.

AVERY. You're / just…

MAXWELL. Okay.

AVERY. Thanks. Now. I'm sure glad you guys had a chance to see that sniper's nest. Hide. And you're working on this escape plan.

TAGGART. We think…Well, I'm in Mr. Kling's hands / on that.

KLING. He'll be fine. He'll be fully credentialed.

AVERY. Good. / Good.

TAGGART. According / to…

KLING. He'll walk right out. It's simple.

TAGGART. I'll need a suit.

KLING. A suit?

TAGGART. Yeah. I should have a suit.

KLING. You don't have a suit?

TAGGART. I have *suits*. I just don't – I'm not the kind of guy that spends a lot of money on suits.

KLING. Whatever suit you have is / fine.

MAXWELL. I assume you're done with me. If you don't mind, I'll leave you to discuss your *escape* plan without me.

AVERY. Oh. Okay. Thank you, Kit. I'll be in touch about getting together one more time, to…to finalize things.

   (MAXWELL exits.)

TAGGART. Ouch.

KLING. I have to tell you, Tom, he's a little unsettling to me.

AVERY. Don't – It's all a little nerve-racking, but the meat of the plan is the rocket. Let's just talk about the rocket.

KLING. All right. We need to cut a hole in the window.

TAGGART. Wait. I was mentioning the suit.

KLING. What's with the suit?

TAGGART. I have cheap suits.

KLING. So?

TAGGART. I should have a better suit.

KLING. Why do I think you just want us to buy you a suit?

TAGGART. I *do* want you to buy me a suit. I have to build / a *character.*

KLING. No. I mean, you need a suit for *this,* or you just want a nice suit?

TAGGART. You can buy me a missile launcher, but you can't buy me / a suit?

KLING. Who's going to notice your suit?

TAGGART. *You know.* Right? Because you're the trained professional. Not me.

AVERY. Just buy yourself a suit, Tag, and give me the bill. And no one is questioning your / know-how.

KLING. Well, wait. What kind of suit are we talking about?

TAGGART. Brooks Brothers?

KLING. Okay.

AVERY. So let's talk about this window.

TAGGART. I can score a circle in the glass ahead of time. With the cutter.

AVERY. Okay.

TAGGART. Then I can knock it out at the last second.

KLING. But there'll be guys watching from the roof.

TAGGART. It's all in the timing. It's got to be fast.

AVERY. Do you need someone up there with you?

TAGGART. I'm a lone wolf.

(*pause*)

AVERY. Okay.

TAGGART. I've got time. As long as the guy stays in the room…And that's where *your* man helps…

AVERY. Is Kit up to this, do you think? After all?

TAGGART. I don't know, you know? I'm still a little concerned about his commitment.

AVERY. It's not enough that he's willing to *die* for this?

TAGGART. That's a big deal, I know. But it's like he wants to
get away with it, too. Like he doesn't want anybody to
know what he did.

KLING. That's what *I* said. Exactly. I was just / saying that.

TAGGART. Yeah.

AVERY. Why should that make a difference?

KLING. It doesn't.

TAGGART. I think it does.

KLING. ...As long as we don't honor his wishes.

AVERY. What?

KLING. We've got to pin this on *somebody*. We have the
resources to put the whole plot on him, and erase ourselves from the picture. Was I crazy to think we were
on the same page on this?

AVERY. Yes. You were crazy to think that.

KLING. What difference will it make to *him*?

AVERY. If what you've said about him is true, then it's a
complete betrayal of his wishes.

KLING. I just said that it was. So what?

TAGGART. He couldn't have got away with it anyway.

AVERY. Why not?

TAGGART. Forensic evidence. It'll come out with or without
us.

AVERY. There will be evidence?

TAGGART. Well, yeah. The place isn't gonna just evaporate.

KLING. See? It can't be helped. So we might as well start
planting the seeds.

TAGGART. Start a paper trail, or something, that leads to
him. Put his fingerprints on some of our work...

KLING. Wipe off our own.

TAGGART. If you will.

KLING. Can't be helped, Tom. Move on.

AVERY. I just don't want to play the Judas.

KLING. You won't be, Tom. You know why? Because, A: Jesus was still alive at the time, not *dead*. And B: Unlike Judas, *you're* going to get away with it.

AVERY. But Judas didn't *try* to get away with it.

TAGGART. Yes, he did.

KLING. *(to TAGGART)* Please.

AVERY. That's something that's been bothering me for a long time. Sometimes I think we should just do this thing, and then step up and say, "*We* did this. We did it, / and here's why."

KLING. Whoa whoa whoa. W– W– Nobody needs to know *why*. They'll know *why*. No *spokesman* is required.

AVERY. Don't worry. I don't have the courage. That's one thing Judas has on me.

KLING. Tom…

TAGGART. Judas *tried* to get away with it.

KLING. Tag, please. Thanks for trying to help, but that's not the point and also it's stupid. / Tom…

TAGGART. He *did*.

KLING. No, he didn't. Judas did not try to "get away" with it.

TAGGART. Yes, he did. Look at the story.

KLING. I've looked at the story. Plus I've seen about a hundred movies on the subject, and he never tries to "get away" with it.

TAGGART. They don't know what they're talking about.

KLING. Is that right, Tag? Or could it be, no offense, that biblical scholarship is just a bit beyond your reach?

TAGGART. Okay, listen. Are you listening?

KLING. No.

TAGGART. Listen:

KLING. Tag, / for…

TAGGART. They're in the garden, right? Jesus and the apostles. Judas shows up with a bunch of soldiers and they're hiding in the woods or whatever, okay? These soldiers / don't know Jesus…

KLING. I know the story.

TAGGART. Hold on.

AVERY. I don't see / the point of this.

TAGGART. Hold on. They don't know Jesus; they've probably never heard of him. They're running an errand. From Herod or somebody, right?

KLING. So what?

TAGGART. So they're like, "Now, when we get in there, how do we know which one is Jesus?" And Judas says, "I'll tell you what: I'll greet him with a kiss, and that'll be the guy."

KLING. So?

TAGGART. So, it's *obvious.* He wanted to get away with it. Otherwise, he would just walk in and say, "Over here. Here's the guy, right here. Yeah, this one." Why wouldn't he? Why wouldn't he do that?

(pause)

KLING. I don't know.

TAGGART. Nothing else makes any sense. See? Instead, he thought he could go in there and give the secret signal, and when the soldiers show up, he'd be like, "Oh, *no. Soldiers.* Where did *they* come from? Oh my god, you guys."

KLING. But that's not what happened.

TAGGART. Because he immediately got busted. Jesus was like, "Hm, I guess you didn't see those *soldiers* on the way in, huh, kissy-face? What am I supposed to be, an idiot? I can see that you betrayed me with that kiss."

KLING. They probably came in too soon.

TAGGART. Yeah.

KLING. Shoulda given him a few minutes.

TAGGART. Yep.

KLING. Holy shit.

TAGGART. It's incredibly obvious. Judas wanted to get away with it.

KLING. *(impressed)* Wow. You're right. You have to be right. You hear that Tom? Judas…uh. Judas. Was not… *braver…*than you. *(to* **TAGGART***)* Was that our point?

TAGGART. Judas was a pussy.

KLING. That can't be our point.

AVERY. Why did he do it, then?

TAGGART. For the *money*.

KLING. But...but...You know, Tom. If he had gotten away with it...we might never know who the betrayer had been. And because he was one of the apostles, he'd probably be a *saint* now. Saint Judas. Get it?

AVERY. No.

KLING. All you gotta do is get away with it.

TAGGART. *Pope* Judas, even.

KLING. Judas – "Our Judas Of..."

AVERY. Let's all just stop saying "Judas," okay? And let's not question Kit's commitment.

TAGGART. All I was saying is that he appears to be...of two minds. And you've gotta be...

KLING. Of one mind.

TAGGART. Yeah.

AVERY. Well, then, I'm asking you: Is he up to it?

TAGGART. I don't know, you know? Nobody's expecting action in the *room*. And from *him*, you know; he doesn't look the part. So there's the element of surprise. And even if he doesn't make it – even if they blow him to pieces before he gets out of his chair – *still*, he's a distraction. For those ten seconds, they won't be taking radio calls from the roof. They'll probably pin their own guy to the floor, which is great. Who knows? It's ten seconds. If he doesn't freak out early, there's no downside.

Truth be told, that's probably all he is.

AVERY. What.

TAGGART. A distraction.

AVERY. I see.

End of Scene

Scene Four

(An anteroom. **FLETCHER** *waiting.)*

*(***MAXWELL*** *enters with the Proposal.)*

MAXWELL. Well? I only have a minute.

FLETCHER. I'm surprised you saw me at all.

MAXWELL. Is this what you want?

FLETCHER. I don't need it back. I have plenty of copies.

MAXWELL. Take it anyway. Save a tree.

(He tosses it onto a table.)

So what *do* you want?

FLETCHER. I want to hear it from your own mouth. Did you have me barred from that meeting?

MAXWELL. Yes.

FLETCHER. I never would have guessed you could stoop so low.

MAXWELL. Now you know. Is that it?

FLETCHER. Are you so terrified of another idea? You couldn't let me stand or fall on my own? You had to play dirty?

MAXWELL. It's how I got to be the man I am today.

FLETCHER. I'm a "security risk." A "*SECURITY RISK.*" Do you hear what that *sounds* like?! For you to *call* some-one…pick up a phone… / and say "This guy…I don't know about this guy…"

MAXWELL. This is what happened. This – I *don't* know about you, / frankly, I don't know about you.

FLETCHER. WHAT?! How can you say this?!

MAXWELL. Who the hell are you? Where do you come from? You're – There are places you don't belong. You should never have been there in the first place. It's just a good / thing I was the one to notice.

FLETCHER. How dare you. How dare you. A "Security Risk"? You've *humiliated* me. / You've…You've…

MAXWELL. Oh, stop it. Are you *so* naive? Or do you re-apply that turnip smell every morning after your shower? What do you *want*, Fletcher?

FLETCHER. I want some *respect.*

MAXWELL. Well, join the goddamn club. You think *I'm* respected? Do *you* respect me? / You come to me…

FLETCHER. Please…

MAXWELL. You come to me in your superior manner…Full of condescension for me and my – You think I don't know / when I'm being condescended to, you –?

FLETCHER. I'm not gonna…I'm not gonna…

MAXWELL. Let me tell you something, Fletcher, there's a time when we all dream of saving the starving children of the world.

FLETCHER. So, why don't we?

MAXWELL. We figure out that there are other ways of being liked.

Look, I'm doing you a goddamned favor. Trust me, you'll thank me for it someday.

(**FLETCHER** *picks up the Proposal.*)

FLETCHER. I'll thank you *now.* But if you think I'm gonna just go away, / just because you feel dried up and… and…inadequate…

MAXWELL. Alright, hold on, now. Hold – Let's not be…psychological. I can still help you.

FLETCHER. I can do without your kind of help, sir. / You've helped enough.

MAXWELL. Now, now, wait. This kind of help you can use, indeed. I have had it copied, this Compromise of yours. I'm sure you won't mind. And I will send it out for you, to a number of people. People you desperately want to reach. Anybody can hire a messenger, right? But if it came from *me*, now…*well.* that's an eye-opener, wouldn't you say?

FLETCHER. Why would you?

MAXWELL. This is not an endorsement, mind you. I'll just say, "Well…I've looked at this document, and maybe… maybe you'll find it of some interest."

FLETCHER. And did you?

MAXWELL. Did I what?

FLETCHER. Look at it? Did you even look at it?

MAXWELL. I...I *looked* at it. I...Oh, now, why spoil it? I'm trying to do something for you.

FLETCHER. Then get me back in the room, for chrissake. Get me back at the table.

MAXWELL. No.

FLETCHER. Why not?! What are you so afraid of?

MAXWELL. It's none of your goddamn business. Now, I've made you an offer. Take it or leave it. I'm running late.

FLETCHER. I'll leave it.

MAXWELL. What?

FLETCHER. I don't want your help. There's something wrong with you. You can't be trusted.

MAXWELL. Well, I...Well, isn't / that a...

FLETCHER. Now if you'll excuse / me...

MAXWELL. Wait, wait. Goddamnit. Sit down. Mr. Fletcher. Please sit down.

FLETCHER. Quickly, please. I have appointments, too.

MAXWELL. Oh, for the love of...Listen, Allan. I tell you you can trust me.

FLETCHER. Fine. If you could give me a letter, of some kind, a letter of introduction, and a list of people you / would like me to send the Proposal to...

MAXWELL. Allan, no. I don't need your *permission.* I'll send whatever I want to whomever I want. I'm just telling you what I'm doing for you.

FLETCHER. You want to *do* something for me? *Read* this!

MAXWELL. Oh, come on! You think I don't know boiler-plate when I see it? A bunch of old treaties stitched together, with the names and dates whited out and re-typed by a junior partner?

FLETCHER. As I don't have a junior partner, you've managed to flatter me and insult me at the same time.

MAXWELL. Well, then, you're welcome and I'm sorry. But this thing isn't worth the paper it's printed on and you know it. It's unenforceable.

FLETCHER. It's an important symbol.

MAXWELL. A *symbol*? Is that what it comes down to? You think *my* side hasn't got symbols? We'll *bury* you in symbols! We'll *drown* you in symbols!

FLETCHER. Can't you just get out of the way? Don't you have enough? Don't you think I know what you're up to? All of you? With your...

MAXWELL. What?

FLETCHER. Your *bullshit*...about...preserving values, and...

MAXWELL. What are we up to?

FLETCHER. It's *greed*. It's just pure *greed*.

MAXWELL. Don't be an ass, Fletcher. I've never been greedy. Greed is for children who...who *need* things. Sad children.

FLETCHER. It *is* sad.

MAXWELL. / But...

FLETCHER. *Whatever* you call it.

MAXWELL. Maybe. Listen. Maybe it's sad but it isn't greed and you might as well know. It might save you a lot of grief, you know? Just to know. How people are.

FLETCHER. I know how people are. I'm actually an adult person, believe it or not. / This is not...

MAXWELL. Hold on, will you? / I've done a lot...

FLETCHER. We're not gonna have another nice sit-down, okay? I'm not gonna indulge you anymore. I have work to do, and I'm tired of this bullshit.

MAXWELL. Don't be stupid, Fletcher. You should always want to know what your enemy has to say.

FLETCHER. Yes. "It's not greed."

MAXWELL. Yes. For example: the Puritans. The Puritans – had no greed. Why'd they hang all those so-called witches, when it made no sense?

FLETCHER. *(dismissive)* I don't know.

MAXWELL. Their reasoning was faulty, any idiot could see it. They couldn't have missed it. Aren't their actions, then, inexplicable?

FLETCHER. They believed in demons.

MAXWELL. How could that be?

FLETCHER. They were…They were operating from / a set of…

MAXWELL. No.

FLETCHER. …A set of theological / interpret–

MAXWELL. No no no.

FLETCHER. Look, whatever it is, it's *sad.* Can we agree on *that?* To have to…to have to carve / your image into…

MAXWELL. Listen to me.

FLETCHER. …everything you see even if you have to kill it.

MAXWELL. Yes. You're right. That's right. But for what fundamental reason?

FLETCHER. For…?

MAXWELL. The thing you just said. Carving our… / image…

FLETCHER. Your– Yes?

MAXWELL. The Puritans: They did the terrible things they did…because to do otherwise…would be to go back to their dull lives. They cannot be reasoned with, because reason is not a factor. They did the terrible things they did for this reason only: Because it was fun.

FLETCHER. Okay. What's your point?

MAXWELL. That you're using the wrong weapon.

FLETCHER. So what weapon should I be using, then?

MAXWELL. My friend: Those weapons have been locked away for your own safety.

Now, I'm going to do this thing I promised you, and that's all there is to it. So if you'll excuse me…

It's been a great pleasure knowing you, Mr. Fletcher. I wish you the best of luck in all your future endeavors.

(**MAXWELL** *exits.*)

(**FLETCHER** *stands holding the Proposal.*)

End of Scene

Scene Five

(TAGGART *and* AVERY)

TAGGART. First, the skin will start to itch. It'll become unbearable, and you'll start to tear your own skin with your fingernails. Then your throat will close up and you'll start to strangle. But – and here's the beautiful part – even if someone could cut open your airway, it wouldn't do any good because within a minute or so your lungs would be Swiss cheese. They would just turn to liquid. They would liquefy. They would liquefy.

AVERY. And how much of this...chemical... / would we need?

TAGGART. Ah, this'd be like...a square centimeter? Like... your thumbnail?

AVERY. For *everyone?*

TAGGART. That would be for everyone in the room, yeah. We *should* use more. To be safe. Considerably more.

AVERY. But you'd kill more people.

I'm just saying.

TAGGART. Sure. But you want to be *safe.* In fact...

AVERY. What.

TAGGART. You might as well use enough for the whole floor.

AVERY. The floor will be cleared of...

TAGGART. ...Innocent...

AVERY. Well. Uninvolved...

TAGGART. Uninvolved persons, anyway. So to be *safe...*

AVERY. Mmhm.

TAGGART. In fact...

AVERY. Yes?

TAGGART. Well, if you're in the building at *all* that day...

AVERY. That's true. You would have to have *some* awareness...

TAGGART. They would have had to *clear* you, if / nothing else.

AVERY. That's true. So you couldn't *not know*. That you were taking a calculated risk.

TAGGART. So I wouldn't take any chances.

AVERY. The whole building, then?

TAGGART. I think so.

AVERY. Under the circumstances, yes. I mean, things have gotten even more serious, if that's possible.

TAGGART. Now more than ever, right?

AVERY. Excuse me?

TAGGART. Now more than ever. If not now, when? If not who...? If not us. If not us...?

AVERY. I wonder where Jeff is.

TAGGART. But there is the question of ventilation.

AVERY. What do you mean?

TAGGART. The ventilation system on that floor is completely self-contained.

AVERY. Oh. So you wouldn't be able to contaminate the other floors?

TAGGART. Not without a great deal of effort. But it can be done.

AVERY. I don't know if we have time for a great deal of effort, Tag. I think the whole floor, I mean, the whole floor, / is more than adeq–

TAGGART. Maybe not a *great* deal of effort. It's worth a powwow, I think. Put our heads together...

AVERY. I think let's just stick with the people on the floor.

TAGGART. Sure.

AVERY. I mean, we're not maniacs.

TAGGART. Of course.

AVERY. But you can get enough of this stuff?

TAGGART. Yeah. I have an excellent source.

AVERY. Miles?

TAGGART. No. Another guy. A guy / he knows.

AVERY. Another guy? I really didn't / want this to go beyond...

TAGGART. He's fine. Believe me. This guy is fine. I vouch for this guy.

AVERY. Good God, I hope so. Because he could hardly fail to know where this…this product / has ended up…

TAGGART. No, no. It's fine. He eats our bread.

AVERY. The circle is just getting / so big…

TAGGART. We have to have the stuff, Tom. We gotta get it from somewhere.

AVERY. Oh, I know, I know, but with recent / developments…

TAGGART. It's fine. I'll make sure he understands. And I'll get plenty of the stuff.

AVERY. Just for the one floor, though.

TAGGART. Yeah yeah.

But better safe than sorry, is all.

Yeah yeah. Don't worry.

(The buzzer sounds.)

AVERY. Thank God. I was starting to wonder.

(He presses the button.)

TAGGART. He's gonna love this. This is a million times better than a knife. / A million times.

*(**KLING** enters.)*

KLING. That son of a bitch! That unbelievable son of a bitch! It just got crazy, boys! It just turned into a god-damn shit-storm! I knew the old stiff wasn't up to it! I knew he didn't have the balls! I should have strangled him the minute you told me he was in on this! God-dammit, Tom, I should have fucking strangled YOU! Are you ready for this? Are you fucking well ready for this, you Sad Sacks, you poor fucked dipshits, you *dead men*?! Sit down for this, Taggart. You're gonna want to sit the fuck down for this, and hear what our lousy, miserable lives have come to. Sit down and hear why I *hate* you, I hate you *both*, and, God help me, I hate *myself*!

AVERY. Holy hell, Jeff. What the hell / is it?

KLING. Here it is, suckers. Here's the news: Kit Maxwell, that fucking traitor of all traitors, has screwed us once and for all. He killed himself. He committed fucking suicide. He was found in his bedroom this morning, dead of a self-inflicted *gunshot* wound.

AVERY. That's it?

KLING. That's IT?! That's *IT*?! Isn't that / *enough*?!

AVERY. For Christ's sake, Jeff, have you been living under a rock? We've known this for hours. We're already planning contingencies.

KLING. You *knew* about this?

TAGGART. Holy shit, Jeff, where have you been?

KLING. I've been *in cognito*. Working. / For *this*, you know...?

AVERY. Oh my God, Jeff, you scared the hell out of me.

KLING. Why didn't you fucking stop me, if you knew? Why didn't you / interrupt me and say...

AVERY. I just assumed you knew. I thought you were / bringing worse news...

KLING. "Hey, Jeff," uh, "you / might like to know..."

TAGGART. I thought you were gonna tell us he rolled over on us. We've been waiting all day / for the axe to fall...

AVERY. That's right. For the shoe to drop. For the / axe to fall.

TAGGART. For the shoe to drop.

KLING. But that's exactly what I'm saying, / goddammit. Wait a second...

TAGGART. I thought you were gonna tell us / he sold us out.

KLING. Wait a second. If he killed him– Well, he *did* sell us out, I think that's pretty fucking obvious. / But it's bad enough that he killed himself.

AVERY. But did he confess. That's what / we're concerned about.

TAGGART. Did he name names? / Did he give names and places, that's what we're talking about.

KLING. That's exactly my fucking *concern*, did he name / names. If he's going to betray us...

AVERY. Jeff, we've had our ear to this / all day. If there was a note, or a letter...

KLING. If he's going to betray us by killing himself, / he's almost certainly...

TAGGART. Hold on, man. This is all / we've been doing today...

AVERY. I have people working on this. If there was / a confession...

KLING. Hold on. What people? How big is / this getting?

TAGGART. People who don't / know the story, but...Tom?

AVERY. If there was a *statement*...If there was a / *statement*, Jeff...

KLING. How can they know the...

TAGGART. He killed himself because he was scared.

AVERY. Nothing has surfaced. I have people / who will tell me...

KLING. If they're biding their time...

AVERY. Jeff. I have people. People in a position to know. People who will not keep secrets from me. At this moment, we are safe. At this moment in time...we are safe.

TAGGART. And Jeff. *Jeff. Buddy.* We have a new plan. A *better* plan.

KLING. I need a fucking drink. GodDAMMIT!

AVERY. Jeff. Listen to the plan.

TAGGART. Jeff. We're gonna take out everyone in the building.

(pause)

AVERY. / The *floor*, Tag...

KLING. What?

TAGGART. The *floor*. Everyone on the *floor*, I mean.

KLING. How?

TAGGART. It's basically the same plan. But better. Our guy goes in. The meeting starts: "Blah blah blah, we're

gonna nationalize the blah blah blah," the watch goes
beep – ten seconds. Our guy pulls the handle on the
/ briefcase...

AVERY. Wait, Tag. / Damn it.

TAGGART. Our guy pulls the handle / on the briefcase...

AVERY. No no no. / For the love of –

TAGGART. Wait a second. / He pulls the...

KLING. What guy?

TAGGART. / He pulls the handle on the...

AVERY. That's exactly what I'm saying, Tag. / You haven't
been...You haven't been...

TAGGART. Wait a second. Pulls the handle on the briefcase,
but it's not a knife. It's a *cork*. The cork from *this*...
(holds up a tiny vial)...which is hidden in the lid of the
case. *(pulls the cork)* And everyone dies.

KLING. Jesus.

TAGGART. Just a demonstration. This bottle is empty.

KLING. Thank you. I'm not a complete idiot. What *guy?*

TAGGART. This guy Tom recruited.

AVERY. Tag, I've told you five times. I cannot talk someone
into dying for this. I *have* someone, but he'll never
agree to it. He has to do it unwittingly.

TAGGART. No no. *Wittingly.* That's been the whole point all
along. He must be / *witting.*

AVERY. Damn it, I've told you five / times.

TAGGART. But this is the / *whole point.*

KLING. Why not just put that stuff in the missile?

TAGGART. What?

KLING. Just put that chemical stuff in the missile, and bang.
Two birds, / one stone.

AVERY. There you go. Problem solved.

TAGGART. I can't believe you guys. This is the *contingency
guarantee.* In case the / missile is...

AVERY. Oh oh oh. That's right. He's right. In case the missile / doesn't work.

TAGGART. If it goes astray, or gets / shot down...

KLING. Why wouldn't the missile work?

TAGGART. You've gotta be fucking kidding me! Do we have to go over the same bullshit over and / over and over again...?!

KLING. This was Maxwell's idea. This two-plan idea. Fuck the two plans. / Fuck Maxwell.

AVERY. No, come on. Tag's right. We have to have guarantees. We all agreed on that. With or / without Maxwell.

TAGGART. The two-pronged attack is the whole thing. The safety net is, is critical... / to the...

AVERY. Right. Of course. We just need to talk to this guy, get to know him a little bit, and figure out how to *dupe* him, to put it bluntly, into triggering this...uh, mechanism, or whatever / it ends up...

TAGGART. Okay, *one*: *I* can't talk to him. I don't exist, remember?

AVERY. Oh, I'll give you an alias or something. / Don't worry...

TAGGART. He'll see my face.

AVERY. Tag, he'll be dead before it matters. Please. With us or without us, he's dead. Now, everyone take one of these...Proposals or whatever they are, and act like you care.

(**AVERY** *hands out* **FLETCHER***'s Proposal.*)

KLING. We're expecting this guy *now*? Tom, this is moving too / fast for me.

TAGGART. ...And *two*: The whole idea is that he has to be *in* on it! What the hell are we supposed to *say*, Tom? "Oh, hey, your Contract is fantastic, now could you just wear this watch and when it beeps, if you could please just take out this little / bottle..."

AVERY. I don't know. We'll *trick* him. If I had a nickel for everyone I've / bamboozled...

KLING. Time bomb. Some kind of little time bomb, Tom. A *chemical* time bomb, chemical *release*, something, / no electronic...

AVERY. Now you're / talking. See?

KLING. ...No electronic parts. An acid, that eats through... a seal, in a specified / amount of time...

AVERY. We *present* it to him, somehow; "Please accept this *briefcase...*"

KLING. *(skeptical)* Mmmm.

AVERY. Oh, crap. But you know what I mean. When we talk to him, something will occur to us.

Right, Tag?

KLING. A watch? A special *pen*, fountain pen, / of some k–

TAGGART. Von Stauffenberg says to Brandt, "I'll be right *back.*" "Watch my *briefcase*; it's got *important papers* in it." "Watch my BRIEFCASE"! "WATCH MY FUCKING *BRIEFCASE*"?! So Brandt moves the BOMB because he doesn't want to kick the important papers with his fucking FEET! "Watch my motherfucking *BRIEF-CASE*"?! You *cocksucker*?!

You need a *man* in the *room.*

AVERY. Objection noted. It's time to move on.

(The buzzer sounds.)

KLING. Who the hell is this? Tom...

AVERY. Everything's fine. Let's just get to know him – and then figure out what we can *do* with him.

TAGGART. But, Tom...

AVERY. Just *improvise.*

(He presses the button. **FLETCHER** *enters.)*

Ah, / Mr. Fletcher.

FLETCHER. Mr. Avery. It's a pleasure / to meet you.

AVERY. Call me Tom. May I call you Allan?

FLETCHER. Of course.

AVERY. Jeff Kling.

FLETCHER. How do / you do?

KLING. Pleased to meet / you.

AVERY. And Mr. T-tag-t...Tarman. Mr. Tarman.

FLETCHER. Nice to meet you.

AVERY. Why don't you have a seat, Allan? Can I get you a drink?

FLETCHER. No, thank you.

AVERY. Really? Nothing at all? / *We'll* be –

FLETCHER. No, thank you.

AVERY. Okay, then. First of all, I'm sure you've heard about the tragedy...the tragedy that the world has suffered today.

FLETCHER. Yes, sir.

AVERY. It's terrible. Just terrible. I know that he was quite an opponent of yours at the end.

FLETCHER. He was very impassioned in his beliefs. I hardly knew him, actually, but he seemed to be a very complicated, very...*(shrugs.)*

AVERY. Mm. You know, Allan, I already miss him a great deal. I had a terrific amount of respect for him. Especially at the end, there. But you know, his...death...has made us reconsider our place in the scheme of things. What do they gain us, our petty desires, here in the shadow of infinity? An idea is worth dying for, sure, but *which* idea? Maybe Kit knew. Or maybe he was just surrendering. But the finger writes, eh? And, having written, moves on. Huh?

So let's get to it. We've been looking at your Summary. We think it shows a lot of promise.

FLETCHER. I'm flabbergasted.

AVERY. Ha ha. No doubt. But there *are* people listening after all. Now you know.

FLETCHER. Well. This is a huge...

AVERY. Well, let's not get ahead of ourselves. / After all...

FLETCHER. No. Of course not. But this is an unexpected reversal. As you probably know, I was even uninvited from the meeting. / Disinvited.

AVERY. Yes. Hm? Yes. I did know. And I think we can reverse that, too. I'm sure you'd like to get back in there.

FLETCHER. I'm not sure that's possible. I was labeled a security risk.

AVERY. Oh, that's nonsense and everyone knows it. It's all politics. I know who to talk to and just what to say. I'm quite sure I can get you back in that room, if you're interested.

FLETCHER. It would mean everything to me.

AVERY. All right. Consider it done.

FLETCHER. Thank you, sir. This is an incredible surprise. A great moment for me, / for this historic…endeavor.

AVERY. Well. Heh heh. Well. We have come to regard your plan as our last, best hope. It's been a difficult struggle.

FLETCHER. Yes, sir. I realize that. May I assume, then, that you'll be sitting beside me?

AVERY. Huh?

FLETCHER. In the room. You'll be with me in there.

AVERY. Oh. Oh. In spirit, certainly. But at this time, this is something best left…You'll have our support, naturally… /

KLING. Maybe you *should* go with him, Tom.

AVERY. Maybe *you* should, Jeff.

FLETCHER. It really would make a powerful statement.

AVERY. Not at this time, Allan. We must be very careful not to appear *too* submissive.

FLETCHER. I certainly won't quibble.

AVERY. And you will be armed with our endorsement, which is…

FLETCHER. Yes.

AVERY. Which is what you've been seeking, after all.

FLETCHER. Absolutely. This is an historic moment. Not to appear presumptuous, but I have the…let's see…the endorsement, with the signature pages, as I always do. If you want to take them, dress them up a bit, for posterity…*(He has produced a thin document.)*

AVERY. Yes.

FLETCHER. And we can arrange a more *public*, more / *official…*

AVERY. Oh, yes. We'll fix these up and, and we'll make quite a show of it. Hooray.

FLETCHER. I assume you'll want to go over some of these issues...*(He takes out the Compromise Agreement.)*

AVERY. Um. Yeah, absolutely. Jeff, have a look at the / endorsement pages...

KLING. Ah. Ah, yes.

AVERY. Mr. Tanman. Mr. Tarnman.

(FLETCHER is leafing through the 410-page Proposal.)

FLETCHER. If you wouldn't mind...looking at Section Five.

AVERY. Section Five. Yes. Mm, I'll tell you what, Allan: We've had a terrible shock today...

FLETCHER. Of course.

AVERY. It may not be appropriate to, to pull this thing apart right now. It's...This is quite a document...

FLETCHER. Yes, it is.

AVERY. I think we should schedule a meeting with all the principals, of our side...

FLETCHER. Of course. I didn't mean...

(Staring at the Proposal, AVERY has an idea.)

AVERY. And... And we could have this *bound* for you.

FLETCHER. Oh, I'm sorry. I'll take care of that.

AVERY. No no no. Let *me* do it. I know just what you should have. It'll look like a volume for the ages. *Jeff* and I will have it *bound* for you.

(Pause. KLING gets it.)

KLING. With a very thick *binding*, right, Tom?

FLETCHER. If you want, that would be...That / would be...

AVERY. Yes. I think so. A very thick *spine*. A very thick, hard *spine*. We could do that. / Right, Jeff?

KLING. *Okay*, Tom. *Yes*, Tom. Got it.

FLETCHER. *(paging through the Proposal)* But I really did – I'm about to leave, but I have to draw your atten– I need y– What the hell...? *This* isn't mine.

(He is lost in whatever he's reading.)

AVERY. Really, Allan...

FLETCHER. I just – I don't understand. Where did th–

    (Pause. He reads.)

KLING. Okay, *where* are we?

TAGGART. *(reading)* Section Five.

AVERY. Allan, we're all going to / meet again soon…

FLETCHER. *(suddenly)* Excuse me, I have to be / running along…

TAGGART. *(reading)* Holy fuck! Holy *fuck!*

FLETCHER. Okay. / Let's keep our heads…

AVERY. *(re: TAGGART's outburst)* / What in the hell…?

KLING. Let me see / it. Let me see. Give me that.

TAGGART. *(to FLETCHER)* Don't move! Don't fucking move! You won't / make ten steps!

AVERY. *(to TAGGART)* What in the / hell has gotten into you?

FLETCHER. *(to TAGGART)* I know. I already know that. Let's keep / our heads.

KLING. *(reading)* Holy / *fuck!* You fucking son of a bitch!

TAGGART. *(to FLETCHER)* You *better* know it. Sit down! *Sit down!*

AVERY. Have you both lost your minds? / What is going on here?

FLETCHER. I'm *going* to / sit down.

TAGGART. SIT DOWN!

FLETCHER. I'm sitting, but we're / going to talk about this before we do anything crazy.

TAGGART. / Sit down! Tom…

KLING. *(reading)* Holy shit. Oh my God.

AVERY. Damn it, someone's gonna / tell me wh…

TAGGART. *Tom…*

AVERY. What. / What is it?

KLING. *(snatching FLETCHER's copy)* He's got it too? He's got it too?

TAGGART. Of course he's got it. Why the shit you think he's / trying to get out the door?

AVERY. Got what? / Got what?

KLING. *(to* **FLETCHER***)* Stay in that chair. Don't move from / that chair.

TAGGART. Don't worry, he's not going anywhere.

FLETCHER. Okay, but we're all gonna have to relax and talk about this.

AVERY. Got what? Talk about *what?*

KLING. *(reading)* AAAAHHHHHH!!!

AVERY. *(re:* **KLING***)* Oh, for GOD'S SAKE!

TAGGART. *(to* **FLETCHER***)* You're a dead man.

FLETCHER. People know where I am.

AVERY. *(to* **KLING***)* Let me see that.

(**AVERY** *takes the Proposal and reads.)*

KLING. *(to* **FLETCHER***)* Why would you do this?

FLETCHER. I didn't know.

KLING. You didn't *know?* You didn't read your own goddamn / Proposal?

FLETCHER. Not since I got it back from Maxwell.

KLING. Not since y– So *he* put this in here. All by himself.

AVERY. What page?

(**TAGGART** *helps him.)*

KLING. He put it in *your* copy, but he didn't tell you.

FLETCHER. I have dozens of copies. This happens to be the one I gave *him.* It's a fluke that I ever opened it again.

KLING. So he gave you this one back. But first, he copied it and sent it to us.

FLETCHER. It seems so.

KLING. And how many of these *are* there?

FLETCHER. I don't know.

TAGGART. Well, how many do *you* have?

FLETCHER. Just this one.

TAGGART. You said you had dozens.

KLING. Tag...

FLETCHER. You don't understand. This is the copy I gave Maxwell. Only the copies *he* sent out contain this page. I had nothing to do with this.

TAGGART. How many did *he* send out?

FLETCHER. I have no idea.

AVERY. *(reading)* Oh, my God.

KLING. Almost up to speed there, Tom?

AVERY. How could he do this to us?

TAGGART. *(reading)* Sixteen. / There are sixteen.

FLETCHER. Listen, gentlemen, this has gone on long enough. There are people who know where I am.

KLING. Yeah. You said that. Just let me think.

AVERY. I just don't understand how he could betray us / like this.

TAGGART. I told you he wasn't up to it! I *told* you / that!

KLING. *You* told him? *You* – Oh, never mind. Shut up. *(to* **FLETCHER***)* Now listen…ah…what th– *(consults cover page)* Fletcher. Allan. Fletcher? I've heard of you. *(to* **TAGGART***)* Don't hover over him. Let him breathe. Now, now, Tom and I…We got these from Kit. And Kit says here that he sent them to all these other people as well. Is this true?

FLETCHER. I'm sure it is. I have no reason to doubt him.

KLING. Okay. Allan, we're going to need you to get these back from these people.

TAGGART. We know who's got them. What do we need *him* for?

KLING. How are we supposed to get them back? We start showing up in people's offices, "Um, can I see that Proposal you got from Kit? The one we've always been ideologically / opposed to?"

TAGGART. Hey. Hello. *You* don't go; *I* go. *(re:* **FLETCHER***)* *He* sent me. *Get* it?

KLING. Why does *he* want it back?

TAGGART. I don't know. It's got fucking *typos* in it. Something.

AVERY. Kit says…he says they've gone to everyone who's supposed to be at that meeting, which means they're all over the world by now. We'll never get them back.

KLING. Nobody said it would be / *easy*, Tom.

FLETCHER. / I have to go. Seriously.

AVERY. They're all reading it right now, probably.

KLING. *(to* **FLETCHER***)* Just hold on. / Just –

TAGGART. He's not / going anywhere.

AVERY. Our names. The dates of our meetings. / The names of our contacts.

KLING. It's not…It's – It's –

AVERY. Every stage of the plan. It's all here on this page. The police could be waiting for us already.

This is his note, Jeff. *This* is his suicide note.

KLING. Wait. Turn on your phones.

AVERY. It's against the rules…

KLING. Tom, turn on your phone. *(to* **FLETCHER***)* You too. You especially.

(All four turn on their cell phones. Silence.)

AVERY. It has to…

KLING. Mm.

AVERY. …start up…

KLING. Yeah.

(The phones begin chiming.)

Check your calls.

(They do. Much beeping. And more beeping. And…more beeping. Then, a pause.)

It's a bluff. It's a bluff, you guys. The answer is, he *wouldn't* do this to us. He *didn't*. He just wanted to scare the hell out of us, because he was a twisted old bastard. Holy God, but he had us going!

AVERY. You're jumping to conclusions, Jeff.

KLING. No, Tom, I'm right. I'm right / about this.

TAGGART. Turn your phones off.

KLING. Right. Right. Turn 'em off. Take his away from him.

TAGGART. *(to* **FLETCHER***)* Let's see what else you got. Empty your pockets. Put everything on this table.

*(***FLETCHER*** begins emptying his pockets.)*

KLING. Okay. If the story was out there, we'd know it by now.

AVERY. That isn't necessarily...

KLING. It's a *joke*, Tom.

AVERY. I know Kit. I *knew* Kit. There has to / be more to it...

KLING. He's trying to...He thinks we'll call it off, I guess.

FLETCHER. May I go?

KLING. Ah hah. That's a great question. No, you may not.

TAGGART. *(re: FLETCHER)* So nobody knows about this but *him*.

FLETCHER. But...

TAGGART. So we can go ahead and kill him.

FLETCHER. No, you can't go ahead and kill me. You definitely cannot *kill* me.

KLING. Tom, if Kit didn't really send this out, then we can kill this guy.

AVERY. He *did* send it out.

KLING. If he had sent it out, everyone in the world would be trying to reach us. It was a joke.

FLETCHER. Of course he sent it out. The joke is that no one will *read* it.

KLING. What's funny about that?

FLETCHER. If you were me, you'd find it hilarious.

KLING. Tom, he's right! Kit sent it, he didn't send it, who cares? Who would *read* the goddamn thing?! He's gotta be right. What asshole would READ it?!

TAGGART. *(to FLETCHER)* So, thanks: We're back to killing you.

FLETCHER. I don't think you are.

TAGGART. You don't, huh.

KLING. Can you do this, Tag?

TAGGART. You bet.

AVERY. *(to FLETCHER)* We're not back to killing you, Allan?

FLETCHER. No, Tom, you're not. No one wants to read this ridiculous little compromise plan. Unless the primary author was to suddenly disappear. If that were to happen, why, this thing would become downright sexy.

TAGGART. Bullshit.

KLING. Hm.

TAGGART. No, it's bullshit. Look at me: "Allan Fletcher's body just turned up? Who's Allan Fletcher? Oh, the guy who wrote the Mumbai phone book? Let me have a look at this thing..." *(He turns pages, mimes falling asleep.)*

AVERY. Well, Allan?

FLETCHER. I was in the room. Then I was kicked out of the room. *Security risk.* Then I *disappeared...?*

KLING. *(horrified)* Oh, Jesus. It'll be a goddamn BEST-SELLER! It's the book of the YEAR!

TAGGART. We can't let him *go.* What are we supposed to do if we let him go?

FLETCHER. You'll just have to run. That's all. / You'll just have to make a run for it.

KLING. No way. / No way.

FLETCHER. What choice do you have? / Your friend betrayed you.

TAGGART. We kill him. We round up these documents. We pick / another guy. We move ahead with the plan.

FLETCHER. I tell you, as soon as you inquire / about this Proposal...

KLING. Okay, okay, listen to me...

FLETCHER. You have to run. Just run.

AVERY. No one is dead yet. / We could weather this...

KLING. Allan. Just listen. *(to AVERY) Weather* it?

AVERY. It's happened before.

FLETCHER. Listen, gentlemen, / I'm walking out...

TAGGART. Sit down! You sit back / down! Sit down!

FLETCHER. I'm walking out / of here NOW!

(As TAGGART and FLETCHER tussle:)

TAGGART. You're / a dead man!

KLING. / Whoa. Whoa!

AVERY. / Tag!

FLETCHER. Shit!

TAGGART. / I will...fucking...!

KLING. WHOA! WHOA!

> (**KLING** *runs to the briefcase, whips the secret knife out and brandishes it at* **FLETCHER**.)

Just sit down, Fletcher, or / I swear to God I'll use this!

AVERY. Oh, my god, Jeff! / Jeff!

KLING. Give it up, Fletcher!

> (**TAGGART** *and* **FLETCHER** *separate.* **TAGGART** *guards the exit.*)

FLETCHER. Don't make it worse than it is, Kling. A man in your position. Look at you.

TAGGART. I just about snapped your neck, prick.

KLING. I don't want to have to use this, Fletcher, but if you don't start to...start to...

> (*The knife is flapping awkwardly on the handle.*)

What the hell is wrong with this thing?

TAGGART. (*vindicated*) Hel*lo. Thank* you.

KLING. (*giving the knife to* **TAGGART**) Take this. This ridiculous –

(*to* **FLETCHER**) Just have a seat. Just sit down. This is beneath you, Allan. I can't keep him from killing you if you're just gonna, if you're gonna, just, *bolt*. Come on. For chrissake. Sit down. Control your hypothalamus. Alright? Sit down.

> (**FLETCHER** *sits.*)

It's time to talk. Get him a drink, Tag.

TAGGART. *You* get him a fucking drink. I'm not the fucking / house boy.

KLING. Oh, my God, Tag. Come on. *Fine. (He goes to pour a drink.)*

TAGGART. I'm guarding / the door...

KLING. *Fine.* Whatever.

Allan, do you even know what we stand for? We've been acting like insane...criminals, I know, because we got a little scared. But we aren't like that. Criminals steal. Criminals attack. We're *preserving*. We're *defending*. Without insisting that you agree with me, can you say that you see the difference?

(**FLETCHER** *drinks; recoils.*)

Is it okay? It's not too strong?

(**FLETCHER** *drinks.* **KLING** *will refill his glass when necessary.*)

From what I hear, you're not so far from us philosophically.

FLETCHER. What makes you say that?

KLING. I understand this Compromise of yours. You just want what's best for us.

FLETCHER. No, I don't.

KLING. You don't?

FLETCHER. No.

KLING. I thought that was your whole...your whole selling point.

FLETCHER. It's bullshit.

KLING. It's *bullshit*?

FLETCHER. Yep.

KLING. Then what *do* you want?

FLETCHER. What's best for *him*.

KLING. What's best for *who*?

(*pause*)

Not *him*? How can you be for *him*?

FLETCHER. Because it's fair.

KLING. *Fair*? Are you out of your mind? You're gonna sit there...Alright. I'm sorry. Alright. Let's not have a whole debate. Just tell me that you understand our position.

FLETCHER. You're murderers.

KLING. No.

FLETCHER. / Terrorists?

KLING. No. *What?!* No. We're vigilantes. This is vigilante law.

FLETCHER. Vigilante law is not the law.

KLING. Vigilante. *Law.* It's "law."

FLETCHER. Well, we could sit here / all day...

KLING. No, Allan. Not at all. I can clear this up right now. You tell me: If the vigilantes are right. If they get the right guy. Mete out the proper justice...Would anyone quibble? Would anyone say, "We need to do this another way"? Of course not. Why would they? Why even contemplate it? Right? You see. So we *don't* have to sit here all day. We've just uncomplicated the argument. We only need to discuss who has *what*...coming to *whom*. Do you see?

FLETCHER. I see.

KLING. Which brings us back to that word you used a minute ago: "Fair"? Tell me, Allan, what, in your opinion, would be "fair"?

FLETCHER. What do I believe in?

KLING. Sure.

TAGGART. Why are we wasting / time with this?

KLING. Hold on. You'll get your chance. I'm talking to him.

FLETCHER. Who says when there's been a crime?

KLING. Huh?

FLETCHER. Get the guy. Mete out the justice. But who decides that he's a criminal?

KLING. *We* do.

FLETCHER. Who are you?

KLING. The ones who have the *will.* The ones who have the *courage.*

We are the victims. We have been wronged. We are the righteously indignant.

I'm telling you to have faith in us, Allan. Have faith in us, and you'll see. You'll see.

FLETCHER. Get me a fucking drink.

AVERY. Get him a drink.

FLETCHER. You're not vigilantes. You're pirates. Seeking plunder.

Now, what is it going to take to get me out of here?

TAGGART. A duffel bag.

KLING. Taggart, *please*. Allan, just let us do our work. It's what Kit wanted. *Despite* this. Why would he go through this complicated, fucking –? Why wouldn't he just pick up the phone and call the authorities: "These guys are doing this stuff…" Wouldn't that have been a lot easier? Why didn't he do that?

AVERY. Because he didn't have the nerve, Jeff.

KLING. Tom. Are you helping?

AVERY. Read what he *wrote*. These people – he's leaving their fate in their own hands. Huh? If anyone actually *reads* this, if anyone *reads* this thing, they save themselves, and Allan is a superstar.

KLING. I am so sorry I asked. Allan:…

AVERY. If they ignore it, they die.

FLETCHER. That is the greatest endorsement this Proposal has ever received.

AVERY. That *is* funny.

TAGGART. Why?

FLETCHER. Because no one will READ this!

TAGGART. But we *did* read it.

FLETCHER. Actually, *I* read it. By accident.

AVERY. That was unfortunate. I think he would have preferred that you read it at *home*.

FLETCHER. Don't be so sure.

AVERY. Really? He tried to save your life once already.

FLETCHER. *Did* he. I don't think s–

(*pause*)

AVERY. I just figured that out / myself.

TAGGART. (*to* AVERY) Where does it say the thing you said?

AVERY. At the bottom, under the, "Let us hold our trials…"

TAGGART. I don't…

AVERY. I mean, not in so many words. / I'm extrapolating...

KLING. Okay, this digression was prompted by a rhetorical fucking question, but thanks everyone. Now, let's get back on topic, huh? Can we do that? Allan, all you have / to do...

AVERY. Jeff.

KLING. *Tom.* All you have to do is walk away. Let us / do our work.

AVERY. Jeff, it's hopeless. He won't agree / to that.

KLING. *Tom.*

AVERY. Don't you see that we're past that? We can't kill him and we can't bullshit him. He's in charge, now. Kit saw to that.

KLING. Tom, I think we can / reason...

AVERY. Oh, Jeff, shut up. If he agrees to it, he'll be lying. It's useless. Offer him something he wants.

KLING. Okay. *Fine. (to* **FLETCHER***)* How much?

AVERY. Oh, go away. Go on. Get him a drink, then, you ass. Give him / something he needs.

KLING. Back off, Tom. We're not going / to let this fall apart now.

AVERY. Goddammit, Kling, where's that knife? I'm gonna stick it in your eye, you hear me? Now stay out of my way.

Tag, get Allan a drink.

(**TAGGART** *does.*)

FLETCHER. You tried to kill me.

AVERY. So?

FLETCHER. Stop calling me Allan.

AVERY. Mr. Fletcher, I would revel in the opportunity to throw my whole-hearted support behind your sage and staggeringly fair-minded Compromise Proposal.

KLING. What?! FUCK his Compromise! I haven't come all this way to lose everything!

AVERY. But Jeff, you're not. You're *compromising.*

TAGGART. He'll never go for it now. He'll turn us in. He'll say whatever he wants now, but as soon as he's out / that door...

AVERY. And there's not a damn thing we can do about it, either. Get him a drink.

(**TAGGART** *refills the glass.*)

But, just out of curiosity, are you going to turn us in?

FLETCHER. *(reading* **MAXWELL** *'s note)* "Let us deal in the open. Let us hold our trials in the full light of day." I'm gonna take that as a last request.

KLING. Emile Zola was a *fag.*

AVERY. Tag, if Jeff speaks again, kill him.

TAGGART. Really?

AVERY. *(to* **FLETCHER***)* Mr. Fletcher, if you turn us in, well, there'll be no compromise. Your man will take everything and, as you know, his triumph will probably cost him his life. As you've known all along. Someone *else* will kill him, probably for the sheer principle of it. And you'll always know you might have saved him.

FLETCHER. Fuck him.

TAGGART. Tom...

AVERY. He's just trying to scare you, Tag. He hasn't made up his mind yet.

Fletcher, if this gets out, there will be repercussions. There will be violence. And that blood – all of that blood – will be on your hands.

FLETCHER. I didn't start this.

AVERY. What difference does that make? Is that fact going to save one life? I can see that you want to do the right thing, but I don't think you know what the right thing is. You just can't believe that the right thing is also the thing that does you the most good. Listen to me. You are a small person. But you have one chance in a lifetime to be a big person. We will sign your Compromise. We will usher you through to victory. All you have to do is join us. We'll put out a new Proposal and everyone will dutifully destroy the old one. You'll be a hero, a famous man. A powerful man. You'll enjoy the pleasures of the palace. And you'll prevent untold misery besides. That's really what you want, isn't it?

FLETCHER. That would be great for you, wouldn't it?

AVERY. Sure. Not as great as annihilating our enemy. But we're compromising. We're *compromising*, Allan. You win.

FLETCHER. I'm sorry, Mr. Avery. But that's too complicated for a small person.

AVERY. Well, isn't that interesting. You got what you wanted and you won't take it. I think I was wrong about you. You *don't* want to do the right thing. We've just made you too angry, you *mouse*. You can't set aside your child-ish desire to punish.

FLETCHER. The arrogance.

AVERY. Of whom? You're blinded by the chance to punish. Blinded even to your own interests. I was wrong to think you'd be dissuaded by the thought of bloodshed. *You* want to kill, too, don't you? You're jealous. Do you want to fire the rocket? Seriously. I'm not speak-ing rhetorically. We'll let you pull the trigger. Feel the blast, the what-do-you-call-it, the *recoil*. You can do that if you want. If you have the courage.

Do you want to fire the rocket, Allan?

FLETCHER. No, thank you.

AVERY. Then, do you want to make a deal? A deal for peace?

FLETCHER. *(shaken)* I can't.

AVERY. Then I guess you've come to the wrong place. We have no use for you.

KLING. So what's next, Tag?

(**TAGGART** *whips off his belt, holds it like a garrotte.*)

TAGGART. Hold him for me.

KLING. Me?

AVERY. We can't kill him.

TAGGART. If it's gonna come out anyway…

KLING. Exactly. At least get rid of the witness.

AVERY. Our story is just, you know, interesting enough. Let's not complicate it with missing children. Huh? But we'd better hide that rocket.

KLING. Hide th– We're RUINED, Tom! Your *old buddy Kit* – has RUINED us!

TAGGART. The plan is screwed. This morning we had a whole plan, and now the plan is Where To *Hide*?! This guy will HANG us!

AVERY. Stop acting like idiots. We never hang. We never hide. We – as I already pointed out – will *weather* it. What have we done, exactly? Bought some hardware, drew up a few charts? Dreamed a little dream? It's not like we screwed our stockholders.

KLING. I'm glad you can be so cavalier. What are we supposed to do now?

AVERY. Start accepting effusive accolades and fielding our many offers, I guess. Jeff, in a few months they'll be paying you and Fletcher here to debate each other at colleges. I'd be surprised if you and I spent one day in jail.

TAGGART. Wait a minute. What do you mean, you and him?

AVERY. Oh, come on, Tag. You can't have everything.

TAGGART. *What*?!

KLING. We can still kill him, Tom. Just on *principle*, goddammit.

(**AVERY** *sees* **FLETCHER***'s AA chip on the table, picks it up.*)

AVERY. Aw, it's his One Year Chip. Congratulations, Allan.

(*He sails it suavely to* **KLING**, *who brightens.*)

KLING. *(to* **FLETCHER***)* Aww, that's adorable, jackass, you want another drink?

TAGGART. No, you guys, we can do this. / Nobody ever needs to…

KLING. I see it, Jeff. Yeah! "This fucking drunk said what about *what*?"

TAGGART. Nobody ever needs to see him again!

KLING. "This fucking…embarrassing guy, got one look at our top-shelf liquor, you know…"? "Started…"

TAGGART. Tom.

KLING. "…knocking back the…"

TAGGART. Tom.

KLING. But we can still put it all on Maxwell! This fucking note – What is it? – It's one little page! We can spin this!

AVERY. Exactly.

KLING. It's nothing! Just the idle ravings of a crazy old, suicidal old, crazy lunatic!

AVERY. Exactly. It's worth nothing. We'll *weather* it.

TAGGART. But wait. We have sixteen names here. Sixteen docu– documents. And nobody's read it yet, right? So they start…uh…

KLING. No.

TAGGART. So these people start having accidents, right? We can get these back, then. / We have…

KLING. No. It's too late / for that…

TAGGART. No. Wait. We have until April twelfth. / We get rid of these guys…

KLING. No. We can't. This asshole knows everything.

TAGGART. That's what I'm saying. We kill him, / we kill these guys…

KLING. Tag. It's already too late. That's what I'm trying to tell you. *(to* **FLETCHER***)* But understand this, Fletcher: When you're in your fucking padded cell after we've dined, after we've *feasted* on your sanity, that fucker will die. Know that that will be us who did that. You…

TAGGART. Okay, *I* know what's best. *I'm* the ops guy! *I'm* the guy in the bubble!

(**TAGGART** *leans in, placing a hand flat on the table.*)

KLING. But we can do this, Tom. You're right.

TAGGART. I'm gonna kill him, you assholes. / I've decided.

KLING. Wait, now. / Tom…

(**FLETCHER** *picks up the 410-page Proposal.*)

TAGGART. No, wait. *I* decide. These are the kind of deci–

(**FLETCHER** *brings the Proposal down hard on* **TAG-GART**'s *hand.* **TAGGART** *is stunned by the pain.* **FLETCHER** *smashes the Proposal across* **TAGGART**'s *head.* **TAGGART** *collapses in pain and shock.* **FLETCHER** *escapes, still clinging to the Proposal.*)

(**KLING** *and* **AVERY** *watch the whole thing in stunned silence.*)

AVERY. /Oh, my God.

KLING. Holy shit, Tag.

TAGGART. Stop him! / Stop him!

AVERY. Don't exert yourself.

TAGGART. Jesus. Thanks for the backup, you guys.

AVERY. Is it broken?

TAGGART. I can still catch him.

AVERY. Don't. He has appointments to keep. Put some ice on that.

TAGGART. That Proposal thing…

KLING. Yeah, it's just too big. But Tom, I see this now.

TAGGART. Listen to me:

AVERY. Tag.

TAGGART. Listen:

AVERY. Tag! We've heard enough from you today. Why don't you shut up now and let the grown-ups talk?

TAGGART. What?

KLING. But Tom, you're right. We do what we always do: *Deny deny deny.*

AVERY. Exactly.

KLING. "Miles *who?*" "Kit *who?*" "Taggart *who?*" / See?

AVERY. Well, not "*Kit* who." We can't pretend we / didn't know Kit…

KLING. No, but… "Kit said *what?* The dead guy said *what?*" "Let me…"

AVERY. Right.

KLING. "We should ask him about that. Oh, he's *dead.* I see."

AVERY. Yes.

KLING. "Fletcher says *what,* the drunken prick? I don't know, he was kind of hittin' the sauce, you know? Enjoys a drink, *doesn't* he? Maybe he's, uh…" I don't know. See?

AVERY. "I can't comment on an ongoing investigation."

TAGGART. / Please, Tom.

KLING. Exactly! Deny deny deny. We'll ride right over this. "These malicious allegations are completely unfounded."

TAGGART. I can *catch* him.

AVERY. "The work of a…"

KLING. "A conspiracy of…fucking…"

AVERY. We'll *weather* it.

KLING. Yes, we will.

(**TAGGART** *storms out.*)

KLING. And I tell you, Tom, I swear to *God,* when this blows over, when the time comes…

AVERY. Yes.

KLING. When it's the right time. The right place…

AVERY. Yes.

KLING. A lot of people are going to burn.

AVERY. Yes.

(*BLACKOUT*)

End of Play

PROPERTY LIST

SCENE 1

Preset:
Bar or drink cart including:
"liquor" in high-end brand bottles
water pitcher w/ water
ice bucket w/ ice
tongs
club soda, soda pop, other mixers
glasses
bar towel

SCENE 2

Preset:
Bar or drink cart including:
"liquor" in high-end brand bottles
water pitcher w/ water
ice bucket w/ ice
tongs
club soda, soda pop, other mixers
glasses
bar towel
On desk:
vinyl-bound document *(410pp)*

Fletcher:
briefcase containing:
vinyl-bound document *(410pp)*

SCENE 3

Preset same as Scene 1

Taggart:
trick briefcase w/ "rigid" handle *(see diagram)*

SCENE 4

Maxwell:
vinyl-bound document *(410pp)*
w/ Maxwell's page inserted

Fletcher:
briefcase

SCENE 5

Preset same as Scenes 1, 3, add:

3 vinyl-bound documents *(410pp each)* w/ Maxwell's page inserted
trick briefcase w/ "folding" handle *(see diagram)*

Avery, Kling:
cell phones

Taggart:
cell phone
small vial w/cork

Fletcher:
wallet
comb
money clip
money *(bills and change)*
key ring w/ keys
handkerchief
pen
breath mints
cell phone
AA "one year" chip

Briefcase containing:
vinyl-bound document *(410 pp)*
w/ Maxwell's page inserted
14-page document

MEN OF TORTUGA - KNIFE BRIEFCASE

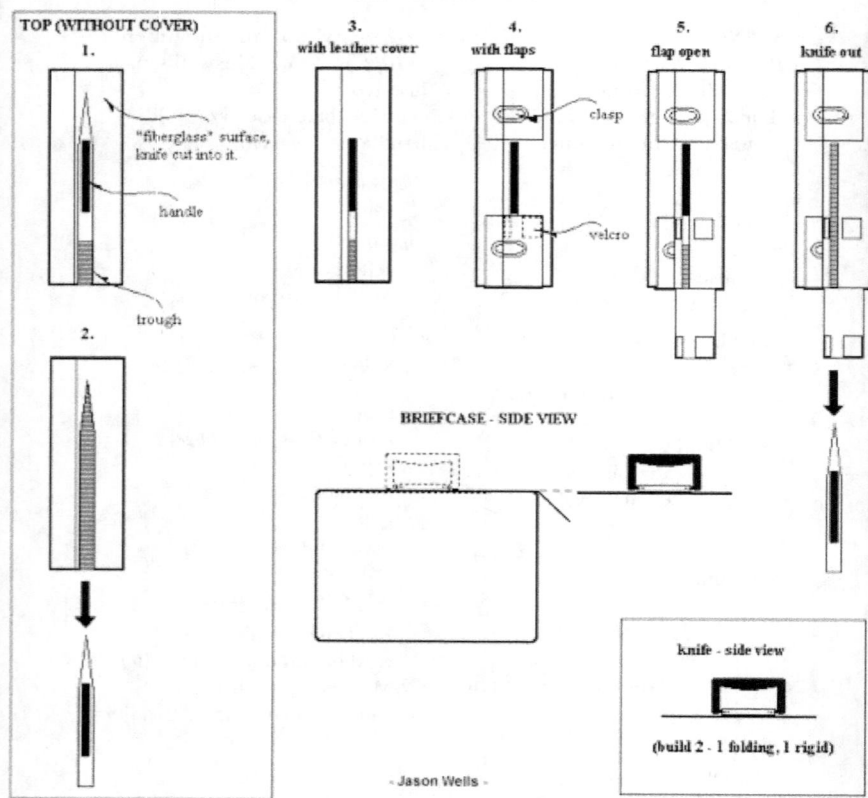

TOP (WITHOUT COVER)

1.

"fiberglass" surface, knife cut into it.

handle

trough

2.

3.
with leather cover

4.
with flaps

clasp

velcro

5.
flap open

6.
knife out

BRIEFCASE - SIDE VIEW

knife - side view

(build 2 - 1 folding, 1 rigid)

- Jason Wells -

From the Reviews of
MEN OF TORTUGA...

"Jason Wells isn't giving everything away in his captivating new play *Men of Tortuga*. In addressing some serious contemporary issues, he creates a scenario where the audience has only a rough idea of what's going on. And that's just about the way it should be. In a crackling world premiere at the Asolo Repertory Theater, Wells tells a story of corporate greed, power, surveillance and the secrecy that increasingly pervades our daily lives. Wells and the Asolo cast grab the audience from the start...The play pulses with energy..."
- Variety

"Calling all corporate conspiracy theorists: Jason Wells has written a play confirming everything you've ever wanted to believe about what goes on behind the frosted windows and code-locked doors of America's executive suites...ripping, blacker-than-black satire...Wells' work, though almost blank in details, carefully exposes the barbarism encoded in corporate bureaucracy. With a grand sense of humor about misinterpreted metaphors and think-tank buzz language – 'he eats our bread' refers to someone you can trust – Tortuga gives us absurd savages in suits, drinking good bourbon and plotting destruction...Eat their bread."
- Time Out Chicago

"Consider an interlude in Jason Wells' *Men of Tortuga*, a tale of global politics, male power games and moral ambiguity that is in many ways the [Steppenwolf First Look] festival's most dazzling and provocative play...When, [the actors] put the final beat on a particularly brilliant scene, there was no stopping the burst of applause. Not only did this crackling exchange work on a slew of levels at once – with matters of ethics, careermaking, legacymaking, ego-massaging, cutthroat cross-generation competition and hints of father-son tensions all being juggled, but the actors attacked the material as if they were playing virtuoso dueling violins. The rhythms, the emotional shadings, the teasing tones, the mix of respect and defensiveness were all so superbly calibrated that they generated a sensation of sheer giddiness...Wells' play happens to be a shrewd piece of gamesmanship that blends a bit of Mamet and his corrosive comedy with a touch of Kafka and Joseph Conrad, plus a splash of high entertainment. It's tailor-made for the age of terrorism, assassination, and corrupt global organizations...with writing and acting this smart and this sharp, it never fails to hit its target....hard-driving, blackly comic, relentlessly macho... [A] 100 minute head game filled with vacuum-packed scenes...Wells has crafted a taut, cleverly orchestrated piece about power, personal psychosis, game-playing, morality and the terror of failure...a sharp parable for our time."
- Chicago Sun-Times

"...Gripping...You'll be hearing more about *Men of Tortuga*, a blistering new play about corporate and government malfeasance from a Chicago actor named Jason Wells (who turned in the best piece of writing all year from a playwright.)...On one level, Jason Wells' elliptical drama *Men of Tortuga* is a genre-based thriller a la James Bond or Quentin Tarantino. But Wells is sufficiently skilled to dig deeper than that...taut sophistication..."
- Chicago Tribune

"...distinguishing itself from its genre [not just] by the author's concise skewering of fundamentally humane civil servants' progress from metaphorical warfare to primitive tribalism, but also through his clever employment of stichomythic dialogue delivered at Mametian warp-speed."
- Windy City Times

"...the testosterone-rich quintet ripping apart the stage (literally) in *Men of Tortuga* makes the lads of *Glengarry Glen Ross* look like delicate hothouse flowers...brutally hilarious thriller...this twisted tale escalates to deliriously wonderful heights of violence and absurdity....Wells parcels out the story sparingly, keeping the audience on a need-to-know basis. It's a method that works perfectly in creating an environment that's at once profoundly ominous and patently ridiculous."
- Examiner.com